Praise for Two Weeks of Summer

"Sweet coming-of-age tale."

— *KIRKUS REVIEWS* (RECOMMENDED BOOK)

"While the emotions are resonant, the gentle humor and brisk prose give *Two Weeks of Summer* an appealingly light touch. All the characters are well etched and engaging, presented with empathy and, at the novel's best, a playful sense of surprise ... This bright, feel good novel about sisterly love, female friendships, and the meaning of family offers heaps of heart."

— *BOOKLIFE* (STARRED REVIEW)

"No matter how things seem on the outside, everyone struggles with something on the inside. Author Katherine Tirado-Ryen brings this reality to light in a way that is not only realistic and fresh, but is also a joy to read ... Characterization is organic and effortless ... *Two Weeks of Summer* is a touching read with the poignant message that love starts within."

— *INDIES TODAY* (STARRED REVIEW)

"*Two Weeks of Summer* is a tale that invites reflection on life choices, personal growth, and the intricacies of familial bonds ... Tirado-Ryen crafts a story that reverberates with authenticity and tender moments, offering readers a heart-warming narrative that shows the significance of embracing change and stepping into the uncertainty of an evolving future."

"Many women will relate to Kim Kincaid. We each have stories about cruel treatment by the popular girls in school or growing up in the shadow of a more talented sibling. But even worse is that intense feeling of being alone - to have no one you can count on .... This book is an excellent read"

"A rock-solid chick-lit novel—engaging, humorous, and touching."

Two Weeks of Summer

Also by Katherine Tirado-Ryen

Two Weeks of Summer

A NOVEL

KATHERINE TIRADO-RYEN

MEADOW LAKE PRESS

Printed in the United States of America.

A Meadow Lake Press Book.

Tirado-Ryen, Katherine.
Two Weeks of Summer / Katherine Tirado-Ryen
ISBN: 979-8-9896849-2-2

Published in 2014 by Meadow Lake Press

To my parents
My niece, Savannah,
And to Chris, with love

Prologue

My mother looks about the small shop with a New Yorker's skepticism, her expert eyes gazing at polyester dresses squeezed too tightly into shelves. She fans through rows of gowns, some on sale, some not, which is odd because we always look for items marked off. "No, no," she says critically, pulling back another dress. She can always recognize quality. "I want it to be gorgeous. Something fit for a princess."

"What about this?" asks the saleswoman, revealing an enormous, bright pink taffeta ball gown that Cinderella might have worn had she been on Percocet.

I watch my mother and know she's thinking this woman is judging her for her unsheddable Brooklyn accent and is not taking us seriously. My sister, Dena, and I are used to this. Ever since our father died, we'd become experts at how others view us. We hide our Puerto Rican heritage as best as we can, but one look at my mousy brown hair and olive skin always has people guessing and judging.

Poor Mom. Between her accent and my looks, the people of Little Rock, Arkansas, are always second-guessing us.

"You can't be serious," says my mother, not even bothering to touch the offending skirt. "This is her senior prom. Can't you find something elegant?"

The woman sighs. "I'll see what else there is. But with your price limitations—"

"Just bring us whatever you have," she cuts in.

As the saleswoman stomps off, I move to stand next to my mother. "It's okay, Mom," I say, flushing with embarrassment. "Let's go somewhere else."

"No," she grounds out. "This is where all the mothers bring their daughters. They're not too good for us." Then, under her breath, "*Carrajo coñyo.*"

Carrajo coñyo. My first Spanish phrase. It means something like "fucking shit" and when I heard my mother say it when she burned her hand on the stove when I was six, I repeated it proudly. My mother had sighed, looking down at her non-fluent daughter who would never learn Spanish because her husband—a dark-haired, dark-eyed half-Puerto Rican—was ashamed of his heritage in an English-speaking country.

"If you're going to say it," she said, "say it right. Roll your r's, *hija.*"

"I can't."

"Like this." And her tongue marched a fandango on her palate.

"*Carrajo coñyo,*" I said, exaggerating the R and laughing at myself.

"*Bueno,*" she said proudly. "Now, here is a dog. *Perro...*"

"This one?" offers the saleswoman, holding between her arms a midnight blue, floor-length gown with shiny blue sequins and a halter neck. One look at my ecstatic face and my mother nods approvingly.

In the dressing room, I slip it over my shoulders and it falls to the floor like rain. I move and the blue sequins shimmer like light on fresh snow. But when I see the price tag, my heart falls: $360. A lot of money for my single mother who's also trying to put my sister through Rice University.

When I step out, my mother's eyes fill with tears. "Oh, honey. You look beautiful!"

"Yes, lovely," says the saleswoman, clicking her tongue.

But I cannot smile, because I know my mother will take the words back when she finds out the cost, demanding something cheaper, with fewer sequins. Something not as perfect.

"What's wrong, Kimmy?" she asks, looking concerned. "Don't you like it?"

"I love it," I say, but I'm tortured because I know I'll eventually have to return this gorgeous piece to its hanger. Sighing, I walk over to her and whisper, "But it's too much, Mom."

"How much?"

I wince. "Three sixty."

Her eyes grow a little wide. Slowly, her lips pull into a broad smile. "I don't care. If you love it, we'll take it."

"Really?" I touch the dress, disbelieving. But then I'm shamed by my vanity, and protest, "But Mom. It's too—"

"Do you love it?" she interrupts.

"Ye—yes." I don't think I've loved any dress more.

"Fine." My mother signals the saleswoman. "We'll take it." Then, back to me, "Honey, for you, I'd buy the moon if it'd make you this happy. Never forget that, okay?"

As Mom lines the paper bags filled with groceries along the kitchen countertop, I suspend my new dress, encased in a fabric bag between my arms and bound upstairs. I open my closet and carefully pick up the dress, smooth the bag, and clear a space on the row of hangers.

After hanging it up, I unzip the bag a fraction, and peek at the incandescent blue sequins.

I cannot believe I have such a beautiful dress. And to prom! For once in my life, things are fitting together. True, I may not like my date like *that*, but Derek is sweet and promises to dance, which is all I really need. It's quite a departure from my dateless wonder days of junior high.

I push the painful memories of those years away, instead reverently touching the blue silk between the sequins. *I'm going to look so beautiful.* Perhaps I will even rival my sister.

At length, I return to the kitchen where Mom is reheating her famous chicken fricassee in a Dutch oven on the stove. Steam is filling the small kitchen and I breathe in the heady scent.

"Yum," I say, hugging her. "How much longer?"

"About ten minutes." She kisses the side of my face. "So, are you excited about prom?"

"Oh, yes!" I exclaim, staring into the orange depths of the pot as the pieces of chicken buoy like little white triangles.

"I'm glad you're going with Derek," she says absently. "Your father would have approved of him."

"Oh, Mom," I say, already tiring. "You know I don't like him. I'm just going with him because you guilted me into it."

"That's not true!" She removes the spoon and gives it two firm taps on the side of the pot. "But you know how we feel about you going out with Spanish boys."

Anger's quick to boil. I can't stop myself from saying, "It's such a double standard. You and Dad were both Puerto Rican. Yet you forbid me from dating a Puerto Rican."

"Your Dad was *half* Puerto Rican," she corrects, "and anyway, it's only to watch out for you. You know how they are. When your father and I lived there for a year, I was the only—"

"Yes, I know I know! You were the only wife whose husband didn't have a mistress," I finish for her.

"Right." She nods solemnly. "I went to that hospital party and found no women but mistresses. They shunned me like an outcast. Can you believe it?"

"That was *one* party—"

"It's how they are—"

"That doesn't mean Juan would've been like that!" Ugh, what a pain. I really like Juan Rodriguez. He's far more clever than Derek. Plus, he's kind, and handsome, and knows how to salsa without stepping on my feet.

Mom takes the spoon and points it at me. "It's how they're raised, if they're any kind of Puerto Rican. I was lucky with your father. Very lucky. You would not have been so lucky. We met in Manhattan. There're millions of people there. The odds are better. You're in Arkansas, where the options are slim. Why can't you just marry a gringo and make your mother happy?"

"Oh, Mom," I say desperately. "Can we just drop this? I get it already, okay?"

She gives me a look, then sighs and returns to her pot. "Fine. Just promise me one thing."

"What?"

"Don't marry a Mexican. They're even worse."

I can't stop myself. "Why? Because they beat their wives?"

I will never understand this hierarchy of acceptable Latinos. The crème de la crème are the Spaniards, then Puerto Rico, and some areas of South America, like Argentina. Then follows places like Chile and Venezuela. At the bottom rung—like me not so long ago —is Mexico. I know it's awful and stupid. But that's what they taught us.

"To *start* with," Mom warns. "Just promise me."

"I promise, I promise," I say, just to make her stop. "Can we please just change the subject?"

"Fine." She tastes the spoon. "Mmm. Have you called your sister?"

The good feelings of today quickly evaporate. "No. Not yet."

"Kim," she says, turning down the heat of the stove before balancing two bowls in her hands. "It's important that you stay in touch with Dena. She loves you very much."

I cringe with resentment. "If that's true, why doesn't she show it?"

"She does," Mom insists. "Listen, when you were kids—"

"When we were kids," I interject, spitting out the words like a foul taste. "That was how long ago? A decade? We've changed a lot since then, Mom."

"I know." She passes me a bowl.

I follow her to the table, and we eat for a few moments in silence. "It's just so hard. She puts this wall between us on purpose."

Mom reaches out to take my hand firmly in hers. "Just promise me you'll try. Try to make a better relationship with your sister."

"But she's the older one!" I protest, feeling like I'm nine again. It's this constant dance Mom and I play. No Spanish boyfriends, be good to your sister, her pulling, me resisting.

"It doesn't matter. Like you say, you're older now and both responsible. Please promise me."

"What's with all the promises?" I ask, annoyed.

Mom sighs and drops her spoon with a loud clatter into her bowl. She puts her face in her hands and looks like she's about to cry. The image strikes me like a hammer. Mom *never* cries.

"Mom? Are you okay?" I touch her shoulder. "Mom?"

"You don't know how long I'll be around," she murmurs past her hands. "You don't know. I just want you both happy."

"We *are* happy," I say, wanting her to smile again. "Come on. Don't worry about us. We're fine."

"You're not!" She drops her hands and her eyes are wet. "There's such a distance between you both. What has happened to this family?"

I meet her gaze but find my voice stopped, as if a cotton rag filled my mouth. How can I tell her it's because of Dad? That his death changed Dena? How his unknown debts and selling our big house and Mom taking two jobs turned Dena cold as ice? How she's never been the same towards me?

"It's nothing," I say. Then, to placate her, "It'll get better."

"Promise me, *querida*." She reaches out to take my hands in hers. "Promise me."

"I promise." She looks so sad, so unlike herself, that I'm racking my brain for anything to change the subject. "You really think Dad would have liked Derek?"

There's a strained moment between us before Mom releases me. "Derek is okay," she says, her voice soft and distant. "Honestly, we just want you to be happy."

"I'd be happy with anyone who really loves me," I say, a little self-righteously.

When Mom smiles, there's something in her eyes I don't recognize. "Well," she says. "Sometimes even that's hard to find."

Chapter One

SATURDAY, DECEMBER 10TH, 2005

I open my eyes and it's morning. I'd dreamed about my mother—something I haven't done in a very long time—and the memory leaves me at a loss.

"You okay?" Jared asks groggily. He slings a warm arm over my waist and pulls me close. "You were talking in your sleep."

"What did I say?" I ask, stretching into him. I'm glad it wasn't my usual nightmare of him cheating on me with my co-worker.

"Nothing much. Just a bunch of groaning. Was it a sexy dream?" He kisses the back of my neck and my toes curl.

"No. Definitely not sexy." His lips drop away and there's a long silence as I stare out the window overlooking the parking lot. Frost eats at the corner of the windowpane. Ice splinters across the glass. I shiver.

"Last night was so awesome," Jared murmurs against my neck.

"Really?"

"Yeah. I like it better when you're wasted. You should let yourself go more often."

"Funny," I say, but I know that it's not. I wonder how many

times I've gotten drunk with this man, and if losing count means anything significant. At length, I hear Jared's rhythmic breathing. He can fall asleep faster than anyone I know.

I stretch into his warm chest, breathe in his familiar scent. I love when he stays the night. Even though we've been together for two years, he's yet to say he loves me and won't move in, claiming "a man needs his space." Still, I know deep down he loves me.

The alarm by the bed goes off. Jared rolls over and yawns, then sleepily plods into the bathroom and turns on the shower. Unable to sleep, I reach over and pull open the topmost drawer of the nightstand. I remove a faded picture of my mother hugging my sister and me. Mom took it on Christmas day over twenty years ago in the backyard of our old house. She'd balanced the camera on a bench and set the timer so the three of us—the "Three Musketeers," as she'd affectionately called us—could squeeze into the frame. She'd tickled us just as the flash went off, sending Dena and me into hysterics.

My throat tightens at the memory.

When the shower turns off, I shakily return the picture to the drawer. After a few moments, Jared emerges naked from the bathroom. He's still the most gorgeous man I've ever slept. The sight of him sends a delicious thrill down my skin.

"Well, I'm off to work," he says, pulling on his purple FedEx uniform. "You still on for Maggie's tonight?"

"Sure," I call from the bed.

"I'll pick you up at eight." He leans down to kiss my forehead.

I move to give him a more proper kiss when my cell on the nightstand erupts a ring and I give a start.

He laughs. "Shit, you're jumpy."

"How perceptive." I glance at the caller ID. "It's Jillian. I gotta take this."

"No problem." He reaches for his bag and steps into the hallway. "See you tonight."

"Have a good day!" I say before bringing the phone to my ear. "Hello?"

"I'm in his house!" hisses a garbled voice down the line.

"Hold on." I cover the receiver as I call after Jared, "Care for you a lot, honey!" This is as close to "I love you" as we can get.

But it's too late. The door has slammed shut and I'm speaking to air.

I sigh and drop my hand away. "Jillian?"

"Kimmy, are you listening? I'm in his *house*!"

"Whose house?"

"Adam's! My boss! *Hello*?"

"You're at his house? Is he there?"

"Sort of," she whispers, and I hear bedsprings squeak as she shifts position. "He's in the shower. I thought I should call you."

"Call me? Why?"

"I found a picture of his wife."

I close my eyes and sigh. For the past three weeks, Jillian has been having an affair with her married boss. Though I find the situation abhorring, I am duty-bound as her best friend to be her sounding board for as long as this lasts, which I hope isn't much longer. "Well, that's not surprising," I say, pulling the down comforter over my chilled legs and leaning back against the pillows. "They are still married."

"But listen to this, Kim..." She lowers her voice to a barely discernible whisper. "She's gorgeous."

"Gorgeous?"

"*Gorgeous*."

"More than you?"

"I think so. The bitch."

I rest my arm over my eyes, contemplating this in the darkness. "Why is he having an affair?"

"Because she treats him like shit."

"Right." I pause. "So, where is this picture?"

"It's right here. Beside the bed. I'm looking at it right now."

"That's awkward. Why would he keep it there?"

"I don't know. Last night, her eyes burned holes into my back. It took everything for me not to throw it at the wall."

I grind my teeth. "Is this your first night at his house?"

"Yep. I tell you, this relationship's moving fast."

"Seems so. Now you're his full-fledged mistress."

"What!" Jillian cries, then immediately lowers her voice. "I'm not a *mistress*. I'm his *girlfriend*."

"When you're a married man's girlfriend, I think that qualifies you as a mistress, Jillian."

There's a pause. "Well, I don't like it. It sounds really seedy." Another pause. "Ahhh! I gotta go. He's coming back."

"Okay."

"See you tomorrow, okay? Keep your cell on!" The phone clicks to silence.

Good luck, I think as I snuggle against the warm pillows with my arm still over my eyes, lulling in my half-awake, half-asleep delirium. Just as I'm drifting, the phone blasts a ring and my heart nearly punches out of my chest. I wish I had a button that could instantly end the person on the other line. "Hello?"

"Hey, Kim. Did I wake you?"

The sound of my sister's voice sends gooseflesh up my arms. "No. I was just up." I tuck a hand behind my head and search for words. "What's new?"

There's a beat of silence, and I instantly wonder what I said wrong. Then Dena says, in an unfamiliar voice, "Don't you remember?"

I blink. "Remember what?"

"Oh my god, Kim. *Tell* me you didn't forget."

"Forget what?"

"Kim! I've only left you a million voicemails and e-mails. Jonathan and I need to be at the airport in two hours. We're on our way to your apartment!"

"Today?" I stammer, having prepared myself for their arrival the following weekend.

"You forgot! Jesus, Kim! I just knew you would—"

"No, no," I interject. "I didn't forget. Ha ha. I sure fooled you."

"You're *kidding*?"

"Yeah," I manage, forcing another laugh. "No, I remembered. Seriously. I was just messing with you."

She gives a frustrated sigh. "So then you're ready?"

I pause. "Ready for what?"

"Your apartment, Kim. Is it ready for Summer? Is there anything she can break? Stuff she shouldn't get into?" She paused for an extended beat. "Did you read the manual I sent?"

"You bet," I assured, casting a sidelong glance at the unopened binder Dena had overnighted weeks ago. A section even catalogues the hazardous substances found in most households. One glance had me terrified to drop anything into my kitchen sink.

"So it's ready for two weeks with a six-year-old?"

I gaze across my cramped apartment. Jared's pants and belt from the previous night lay crumpled on the floor, his cigarette butts filled the ashtray by the bed, and my black lace panties and matching bra are in a heap in a corner. I see patches of faded beige carpet through Jared's collected debris. It isn't nearly clean enough by my standards, but Jared didn't care. He just piled his shit everywhere, and I never mustered the time or energy to sort through it. "Yeah. I guess so."

"Okay," my sister says warily. "So then—"

"Dena," I begin, flaring with panic. What the hell am I supposed to do with a six-year-old? My apartment's dark by the time I get off work. There's barely enough time for semi-decent sex before bed—and that's only if I'm lucky. When did I last see Dena's kid? Her fourth birthday party?

Ugh. I'm a terrible aunt.

"What?" Dena calls down the line.

The words burst out before I can stop them. "How do you know I can do this? I mean, Christ! I was the one who offed all our goldfish when we were kids, remember?" Totally true. Mom didn't even trust me to feed Mocha, our chocolate-colored lab. Dena was the one who remembered to fill her bowl with fresh water and chow, take her out for walks, and play with her. I've always felt wary around anything more lively than a potted plant.

"Kim," she says evenly, "the tickets are nonrefundable and we're already here. You said you wanted to be a real aunt to Summer. This is your chance. Just keep to the manual and you'll do fine. Remember, you can always call for my help, day or night. Okay?"

I hesitate. "Okay."

"Okay," she breathes. "We'll be at your place in thirty minutes. Be ready!"

I set the phone down as nausea curdles my stomach. Somehow Dena always gets her way, regardless of how much it inconveniences everyone else.

I sigh as I plod to the bathroom and switch on the light. In the mirror, I catch my reflection. My legs are chubby and short and my stomach pooches over the elastic waistband of my pajama bottoms, making me look like a walking mushroom. My breasts are a sickly white because I'm too embarrassed to sunbathe topless. Long, mousy brown hair frames an oval face with mud-colored eyes. Thin lips frame straight teeth that are yellowing from the cigarettes.

Why had all the looks and bright future gone to Dena? I know that it's terrible harboring all this envy toward my sister, but I can't help it. We haven't been friends since we were kids, and now we're as close as distant cousins. I wonder if things'll ever change between us —and if I even want them to.

I run the water and brush my teeth, then dampen a towel and attempt to scour the mascara that's fused to my skin and gives me the appearance of raccoon eyes. Then I walk into the kitchen and open the fridge, pulling out a half-empty bottle of Absolut Vodka and a gallon of pulp-free orange juice. I mix the screwdriver on the counter next to a row of soiled dishes and beer bottles piled from the night before.

As I chug down breakfast and stare out into the distance, I can't help wishing I were an only child.

Chapter Two

At precisely 12:25 p.m., the doorbell rings and I take in a breath and open the door. Standing before me is Jonathan Nordstrom, my sister's stunning husband who would probably spend the rest of his life as in love with my sister as the day they wed.

"Hello, Miss Kincaid," Jonathan says, leaning in to graze his lips across my cheek as he steps inside. The strap of an enormous pink and white polka-dotted duffel bag bites into his shoulder and he clutches two large Louis Vuitton suitcases. "We might have packed too much. Where should I put these?"

"Wherever. I'll deal with them later." I shift on my heels as he sets them beside my only sofa. "What can I do to help?"

He grimaces as he stretches his back. "Well, Dena could really use your help downstairs. Summer hasn't come to terms that we're leaving her behind." He glances at the enormous Graco box Dena had shipped to my apartment over two weeks ago. "And I'll need your keys so I can put Summer's booster seat in your car."

I hand him the keys and glance down the narrow brick stairwell, spotting my sister by a yellow cab with a suitcase at her feet and a brooding six-year-old in her arms. When Dena sees me, a wave of relief washes over her face. "Kim! Could you come and get this bag? Then I can bring up Summer."

"Don't want to stay," Summer says, crossing her arms defiantly across her chest. Her dress of pink frills would've been darling had her face not collapsed like a grumpy old man.

"Come on, sweetie," Dena soothes, stroking her in a motherly way. "It won't be that bad. Aunt Kim will take good care of you." She throws me an apologetic look as I bend to retrieve the final suitcase. Its weight has me wondering what the hell's inside. All this for a six-year-old? When Jared and I went to Mexico last year, I packed everything into a single carry-on and a backpack!

"Yeah," I say, forcing a smile. "Loads of fun. Promise."

Summer takes one look at me, and her lips completely disappear. She turns her face up towards Dena and the sunlight glimmers in her unshed tears. "Please, Mommy. I promise to be good. I *promise*."

I shudder as I follow my sister up the flight of stairs and into my apartment. Almost immediately, Summer erupts a disapproving, "Ugh! This place *stinks*."

"Are you smoking again?" Dena demands, whirling on me.

"Of course not! It's Jared. I tried to clean as best as I could." All lies. Not only had I polished off the last of a pack earlier this morning (outside), but all I've done to clean was to spray Glade Potpourris into the air-conditioning unit. I figured it's pointless trying to revert the apartment to pre-Jared conditions in a single morning. I've never noticed a smell, anyway.

Dena trades a serious look with her husband. "Jonathan, I don't know. Maybe this wasn't a good idea."

"It'll be fine," he says quickly, looking to me for aid. "Dena, she's your sister. She's your family. Your *only* family. If you can't trust family to take care of your own, who can you trust?"

"Maybe if we spoke to your co-worker again. Offered to pay a little more—"

"It's too late for that."

"But I have her number. I could just call..." She's already reaching for her phone.

Jonathan waves his hands in frustration. "Dena. Be reasonable. We won't make it on time. We'd have to buy a flight home and another flight back."

"But do you think she'll do a good job? Just look at this place!"

"*She* is standing right here!" I pipe in. "And things will be fine. I know it's not the Ritz or whatever, but plenty of kids live in these apartments and I don't hear them complaining." I fold my arms over my chest, proud of myself. Dena hates being referred to as a snob, and anyway, I bet there are kids in these apartments. I just don't know any of them personally.

"Fine." Dena gives an exasperated sigh as she props the window open with a stray black sandal. Her husband is already gone, probably vetting the rest of the house. "Jonathan?"

"Yes?" he calls from the bedroom.

"Do you think we forgot anything?"

"Honey, we checked the house four times. If we left anything, it's probably for the best."

"Right." Dena glances at me as she re-shoulders her blissfully silent daughter. "All the emergency numbers are in the front pocket of the duffel bag. There's also an envelope with two hundred dollars for groceries and a list of what she normally eats. Jonathan bought a gallon of white grape juice, so you'll be set on that." She glances at the refrigerator. "I better put that in now, so it's cold for lunch. Here, sweetie. Move over so Mommy can reach the groceries."

When I collapse onto the couch with its faded blue slipcover, a cloud of cigarette smoke puffs up. Shit. Because of Jared's unwillingness to smoke out the window during the winter, I'll have to vacuum the couch with Viking ferocity.

The fridge opens and Dena gasps. "Summer, go run to Daddy."

Summer slinks off my sister and darts into the bedroom.

Dena levels me with a disapproving gaze. "Where's the food for Summer?"

I blink at her. "What are you talking about?"

She brandishes the near-empty vodka bottle and a half-gallon of margarita mix. "This is all I found, expect for some moldy bread and Chinese takeout. I thought you would have gone shopping before we came so that I could reimburse you. I gave you a grocery list in the manual. Did you even *read* it? Where is it, anyway?" Her eyes cast about the apartment.

"Calm down already." I take the bottles, slide them in the fridge, and return to the couch. "I'll just go shopping later."

Her deep sigh says the lack of groceries is not the end of her tirade. "Can you just promise there won't be any parties while we're gone? I don't want my daughter being exposed to any of *that*."

I narrow my eyes as the unspoken word hovers between us: *trash*. "So now I have to stop my life because you want a vacation? What kind of arrangement is this?"

Dena comes around and sits next to me on the couch. Her nose wrinkles. "I smell smoke."

I wave this comment away. "I'll clean it later."

Dena's face falls. She looks exhausted. "Listen. You know I'm in a jam. I normally would never ask this. Summer hardly knows you, and we all know how inexperienced you are at babysitting."

I snort. "This is hardly thanks, Dena."

She puts up a hand. "Let me finish. Jonathan and I hardly have one-on-one time together between work and Summer. This will be our first child-free vacation in over four years. I didn't know the regular sitter would cancel last minute, or that our best friends would be in Europe. This really means a lot to us. Honestly, I was a little surprised that you even offered."

What was I thinking? I wonder, forcing myself not to roll my eyes.

"But it was a welcome relief that you did," Dena continued. "And I know that in your heart you're a good person. The bottom line is that I trust you. I *have* to trust you." I scowl, but Dena isn't so easily deterred. "Come on, Kim. We're family. We're supposed to be there for each other."

When were you ever there for me? I almost say, but then I remember the thousand-dollar checks she sends me once or twice a year, unsolicited. I sigh, finally relenting. "Fine. Whatever. No more partying until you come back."

"You'll be getting a heck of a present on Christmas Eve," she says, a smile tugging at her lips. "And then we'll take the afternoon flight home and Summer can wake up to Christmas. After that, you'll have everything back to yourself."

"Sounds fine."

"Thank you for this. It's just been so..." Her voice trails. She looks like she is about to say more, but embraces me. I breathe in her Christian Dior perfume and touch her salon-cut, auburn-colored hair. The hug reminds me of when we were kids.

My heart falls. My eyes sting. I pull back before I give myself away.

Dena, oblivious and back to her old self, rummages through her purse. "I know you're busy with work and everything. I did a lot of research and enrolled Summer in an excellent day-care center. It's two minutes from your apartment and the people I spoke to are really nice. Here's the address." She hands me a crisp business card. "I've already pre-paid. You're all set."

I glance at the cream-colored card with its swirly Winnie the Pooh vibes. "Great."

There's a pause as my sister openly regards me. "I've been meaning to tell you to cut down on your eye-makeup. It'll give you wrinkles. Men don't like it. At least not the best men."

"Whatever," I say, not wanting to be lectured on my appearance by anyone, especially my sister.

Just then Jonathan returns with Summer attached like a lichen to the trunk of his leg. "It's time to go, Dena. We're going to miss the flight."

Dena bends down to embrace her daughter. "Bye, honey. Give me a kiss."

"Don't leave," Summer whimpers, her eyes like two enormous white saucers. "Don't leave me here."

I head to the kitchen to fix a drink, then reconsider. I lean into the counter and count the cracks in the linoleum as Dena and her husband say their Webster Dictionary-length goodbyes and finally head out the door. By then Summer squats like a mushroom in the middle of my apartment, hands folded in her lap, eyes downcast.

"Have fun," I call half-heartedly as the door closes behind them.

Almost immediately there comes a muffled cry and I turn just in time to see my niece collapse on the faded carpet, her little shoulders racking with sobs. "Oh my god," I moan, wondering what I'm supposed to do as guilt spreads to the tips of my fingers. "Come on, Summer. It won't be that bad. I promise. We'll have loads of fun."

"I want my Mommy!" Summer chokes, curling into a ball. "I want my *Mommy*!"

I hesitate, unused to her sudden vocabulary and ability to express herself, then walk over to kneel beside her. My memory of her was someone much littler, who could barely stumble through two-word sentences. Now she's reached the age where I'll have to negotiate. "Come on. It really won't be that bad. What can I do to help?"

"Bring them back!"

I roll back on my haunches, wishing I could be anyone else, anywhere but here. "How about some food, huh? Or some TV?"

"I want my Mommy!"

"Well, I can't give her to you!" I snap. Ugh. I'm not good with kids at all. I draw a steadying breath and soften my voice. "You'll just have to accept that, okay?"

"I want my Mommy!"

"That's it," I hiss, standing up and heading to the fridge. I don't care what I promised. Already this experience was turning me into an alcoholic.

I'm about to open the refrigerator when the wails abruptly cease. I freeze, my hand suspended in midair. Then I see Summer stamp around the corner, wiping her eyes with balled fists and looking very irritated. "Why did you leave me?"

I drop my hands, wondering if I was ever this nutty as a child. "I didn't leave you. I was just getting something to drink."

"What?"

I think fast. "Water."

Summer regards me suspiciously and I'm reminded of the look my sister gives when she knows I'm lying. "I want water, too."

"Don't you want your juice?" I reach for it.

"No."

"Why not?" I wave it back and forth enticingly. "Your folks bought you a whole gallon."

"Juice is for babies. I'm not a baby."

I quirk a brow. "Oh, you're not, huh?"

"Nope." Summer crosses her arms across her flat bosom. "I'm a big girl."

"And you think big girls drink water?"

"Isn't that what you drink?"

I hesitate, then nod. "Sure, kid. Whatever." I reach into the cabinet and pull down two pink plastic tumblers. "How much do you want?"

She shrugs, staring up at me expectantly.

I fill both glasses halfway and hand one over. Summer balances it in her hands, watching as I tip the liquid to my lips. She takes a cautious sip, barely enough to wet the tongue of a mouse. I smack my lips together and grin wide as a clown. "Ah, now that's the good stuff."

Summer doesn't look convinced. "It's okay. What's for lunch?"

"What do you normally eat?"

"Calzones."

I let out a laugh. "Do you really?"

"Yes," she says, almost convincing me. "Every day."

"Well, sorry. I'm fresh out of calzones." I think of what's in my cabinets. Not that much. Mom would have been so disappointed. She would have rooted through my pantry, tut-tutting, "Where are your spices? The Goya? The chicken? Do you even have long-grain rice?"

"Mac and cheese?" I offer Summer.

"What's that?"

What is *it?* I'm horrified. What has Dena been feeding this girl? "It's food."

She shrugs dismissively. "Whatever."

"You're just like your mother," I say as I search for the box.

After I retrieve a bowl and start mixing water and the dried noodles together, Summer wanders around the apartment and is gone about five minutes before I've taken notice.

I slide the bowl into the microwave and let it run while I search the various rooms, quickly locating my niece in the bedroom rummaging through last night's stack of lingerie.

"What's this?" she asks, brandishing my black macramé thong that Jared bought for my birthday six months ago.

"Gimmie that!" I rush to snatch the garment from my niece's death-grip. "This isn't for you." I shove it down between the runny hose in the topmost drawer of my bureau. When I see Summer's disgruntled expression, I sigh and ready myself for yet another apology. "I'm sorry, honey. Aunt Kim is just stressed."

Summer crosses her arms over her chest, tilts her chin up, and promptly stomps from the bedroom with an audible *humph*.

Sweet baby Jesus, I think as I stumble after her. *These two weeks'll be the longest of my life.*

Chapter Three

THURSDAY, NOVEMBER 6, 2003

I always smell like beer when I'm at work and I hate it. The Pub has seventy-three taps lining the wall behind the bar top. While some have interesting shapes, like a swan's head and a blonde woman kicking her leg up under her skirt, I've never been able to remember them all. I've gotten good at memorizing the most popular orders and avoid talking about the subject to customers. But some keep pressing me about weird statistics, good brands, and countries of origin, expecting me to be some sort of crazy beer encyclopedia.

"Which do you like?" some random person will ask.

"Fosters!" I'll exclaim with cheerful confidence, having not actually sipped Fosters but loving the Aussie commercials, anyway. It's only a matter of time before I'm discovered. I dread searching the *Want Ads* again.

Not that the job's that great. I'm usually first shift, which pays the least tips, but I couldn't handle a night crowd. It's a job. One that regularly pays.

I'm relieved to finish work and head to my car. It's freezing outside, and I have to slip on my wool gloves and tighten my scarf.

The black pavement is sludgy with old snow and I avoid the puddles and slow my pace.

I turn on my car and heat my hands on the vents. Once my knuckles warm, I turn on the radio and listen to "Stand By Me" on the drive to the mall. Another day, another job. I craved a nine-to-fiver with benefits, but I didn't even have a community college degree. That left few choices.

I park and blow into my hands as I walk through the lot. A warm blast of air hits me as I open the glass door to the mall and I hurry the escalator to the small lingerie boutique. Lynn is practically stomping her foot, and she looks extremely annoyed to see me.

"I know, I know!" I say, trying to look stricken. "Sorry. I won't be late again."

"Don't," she warns, and then furiously slides on her gloves and heads out.

I sigh and take her place behind the counter. A few young girls and older women breeze in and out of the store. An hour passes with only two customers. It's a slow night and I loathe every breath of the rose-saturated air. Who on Earth thinks reeking like flowers is sexy? I sigh and rest my chin on my first and stare dismally at the racks of lacy garters and thongs that I will never fit into, or have any occasion to wear.

I'm staring off into the middle distance when a male voice says, "She looks about your size."

"Excuse me?" I say, my reverie broken.

"A girl I'm seeing," says a man about my age, grinning widely. He's so handsome that I find my mouth has already gone dry. "She's about your size."

My size? He's dating a girl like me? I try to sound casual. "Oh? Do you need help finding something for her?"

"If you don't mind."

I don't mind at all. Anything to break the doldrums of sorority girls prancing about in the changing rooms asking for something smaller, something sheerer.

Her name is Clarisse, and they've dated for three weeks. He says she's adventurous in bed and that he wants something dark and sexy for her, preferably in the S&M league. Naturally, our store doesn't carry such things, but I direct him to the closest thing: a row of satin garters and nipple-free bras. As he speaks, I hang on his every word. I really missed having a boyfriend.

"Thanks for your help..." he says, his voice trailing as he stares pointedly at my name tag pinned just above my right breast. "Kim."

"Sure," I say, then summon all my courage. "What's your name?"

"Jared." He extends his hand. "Jared McKenzie."

I shake his warm, firm hand and then point awkwardly at my name tag. "I'm Kim. Kim Kincaid."

"Well, Ms. Kincaid, I hope to see you around." He grins and hands over his debit card. He leaves with his one hundred and seventy-three dollar purchase in a bright pink and white bag swinging over his shoulder, a gift receipt, and my heart.

Twice a week for two months I wait for him to stroll up to my counter, telling me he's broken up with his girlfriend and that he wants only me.

Just when I've given up all hope of seeing him again, I catch him strolling past the store, pause, and step inside. He pretends to look at a rack of negligees while stealing glances my way, which I return eagerly. At length, he saunters over to my counter and says, "What's your name again?"

"Kim," I say immediately, not caring that he doesn't remember, or even attempts to look at my name tag. "So, did your girlfriend enjoy her present?" I'm normally never so bold, but I know in order to get his attention, I'd have to be.

"What girlfriend?" he returns with a sly grin, which sends a delicious thrill through me.

My cheeks redden under his stare. "Oh. Well—"

"When do you get off, Kim?"

"Eleven."

"How about a drink?" he asks, eyes twinkling.

The single word explodes like a thunderclap. "Yes!"

Chapter Four

I collapse onto my sofa, my head splitting like a cracked coconut, my breathing ragged and my palm armed with three Advil.

I swallow the pills dry and close my eyes. Summer sits in front of the television a few feet away in the miniature purple foldout chair Dena wisely packed. Her eyes are wide with fascination as Cinderella's rags morph into a shimmering silk and satin ball gown complete with glistening glass slippers.

I glance at my watch. 8:30 P.M. It felt like forty hours have passed since Dena materialized on my doorstop. It was hell to get Summer to eat anything and calm her down as to her abandonment, not to mention the marathon task of unpacking her three enormous suitcases.

I'd struggled to drag all the Louis Vuitton bags onto my bed— marveling at the fact that I was touching such expensive suitcases, and that they belong to a six-year-old—and grunted as I opened them to reveal their contents.

"Holy crap," I'd breathed, passing a hand over my sweating forehead. *The kid's got a better wardrobe than me.*

Dena had meticulously set out a year's worth of clothes meant to rotate through the next two weeks. There were mini Capri pants and Gap jeans, cotton sweaters and turtlenecks, leather boots and patent leather heels, a miniature Burberry coat, jewelry, bows, and ribbons. There's even a frilly pink thing tucked in the corner of the second suitcase. I pulled it out and held it to the light.

"My tutu!" Summer exclaimed, bouncing up and down with her pigtails in a whirlwind. "Gimmie!"

I handed it over and Summer hiked the frills over her rump and executed a series of graceless *pirouettes* and *tour jetés*.

The third bag contained salon shampoo, conditioner, detangler, bubble and cream bath, Vics Vapor rub, Children's Tylenol with corresponding plastic measuring cup, a list of hospitals and emergency numbers (I'm surprised she didn't prepare for a malaria outbreak), six different brushes with a set of curlers and a blow-dryer, a month's supply of fruit snacks and animal crackers and a thousand other items I didn't have the energy or interest to sort through. I figure a six-year-old wouldn't care about living out of a suitcase. Or several.

Summer had pointed out the twenty-something Disney and educational DVDs alphabetized in the first suitcase, along with a small DVD player and corresponding remote. I didn't protest when she'd asked to watch one.

A few hours of peace, I'd thought with relief, before realizing there was only one television and—being her guardian—I'd have to watch over my niece in case she got into trouble. There was also the task hooking up the DVD player, with many failed attempts and many, many curse words mumbled under my breath as I huffed around and around the television trying to figure it out before Summer mercifully came to my aid by pushing the wires into the correct inputs. Which only made me feel like a complete and total moron.

I drift off to sleep just as Cinderella arrives at the royal ball. In my dream, Dena gives birth to septuplets and dumps them all on me.

Someone is placing feather kisses on my eyelids. I blink groggily awake. Summer is smiling and I'm seized by the suspicion that something's wrong.

"Hi!" she exclaims. "I woke you up like a princess."

The credits are rolling across the TV. I do some quick calculations and figure Summer had come to me shortly after the movie ended. The relief is palpable and I break into a wide grin. "You sure did, honey. Did you like *Cinderella?*"

"It was okay," she says, then points to the door. "Someone knocked."

"They did?" I sit up and plod over to the front door, squinting through the peephole.

I recognize the sandy hair peeking beneath the stained red Razorback cap immediately. "Jared? What are you doing here?"

"Yo, Kim!" he calls, moving so that his china-blue eyes are inches from mine. "I left my keys on the table. You ready to go?"

As I open the door, Summer races over and attaches to my right leg. Jared takes no notice as he strides inside, setting down a brown paper bag with the throats of two wine bottles peeking over the edge and pockets the set of keys he'd left beside a stack of *Cosmos.* "I called Maggie. She said everyone's there and already getting smashed. It's BYOB, so I bought you some Bacardi Silver. Are you ready?" He finally turns to look at me.

His eyes drop to my leg and the child gaping up at him. "Um, I..." he stammers, as if he's noticed an enormous spider and is trying not to invoke a panic. "What the hell is going on?"

My hand drops to my niece's forehead. Thinking I had an extra week, I hadn't told Jared I was babysitting. I push a hopeful smile into my face as my hand strokes my niece's hair. "This is Summer."

"Who?"

"My niece."

He looks confused. "What's she doing here? Where's her mother?"

"In Aspen. I'm taking care of her."

"For how long?"

"Two weeks."

Jared turns his face away and makes a strange noise. It takes me a moment to place it. "Why are you laughing?"

He catches his breath. "It's just that you're not exactly the maternal type."

My face darkens. "What the hell does that mean?"

"Well, look at this place." He spreads his hands. "Look at *you*."

"What about me?"

He sighs, all humor gone. "Never mind. Let's just drop it."

"No," I say as Summer tightens her vise-like grip. "What exactly are you saying? That I can't be a good mother?"

"Kim, come on. You couldn't keep a Chia Pet alive."

His burst of laugher sucker-punches my stomach. It's true that I've yet to keep a single plant alive in this apartment, but why does he assume I'm the Mistress of Death?

"Anyway," Jared continues. "You getting dressed? You're making us late for the party."

I glare at him, embarrassed that my niece has witnessed our exchange, even though she probably doesn't understand any of it. "I'm not going."

He bristles. "What?"

"I'm not going." I cross my arms over my chest. "You think I'm going to bring my niece to a party?"

"You could find a babysitter—"

"I don't know any babysitters!" I exclaim, wondering how he could suggest something so stupid. "Why the hell would I?"

Knowing he can't win, Jared settles for having the last word.

"Fine, Kim. *Fine*. I'll go by myself and *you'll* look bad. That's fine with me."

I say nothing, only follow him to the door with cold, dark eyes.

He's in the hall before he realizes he left the booze on my vinyl countertop. In a huff, he snatches the bag and stomps out, mumbling, "Call me when you're not PMSing." He slams the door and the pseudo-rosewood picture frames swing treacherously on the adjacent walls.

My eyes pound. Before I can cry, something tugs on my pant leg. Summer's bright, caramel-colored eyes meet mine.

"What's PMS?" she asks softly.

It's strange having her so near, yet also comforting. "It's nothing. Do you want to watch another movie?"

She looks incredulous. "What movie?"

I flip open my mental Disney Rolodex. "How about *Beauty and the Beast*?"

She shrugs. "If you watch it with me."

"Sounds good," I say, and together we slip the film into the DVD player and settle back against the couch.

But I can't stop myself from thinking of Jared. What is happening to us? Why can't he understand? Or is it me? He'd been looking forward to this party all week, and I'd canceled last minute. But shouldn't he be more understanding? Or are all relationships like this? Somehow I can't picture Jonathan, the perfect professor, slamming the door on my sister.

What it's like to be happy?

The question punctures my heart. Aren't I happy with Jared? Isn't he the one? How can I know for sure?

I reach for my cell and speed-dial Jared's number, but after two rings I'm sent to voicemail, which can only mean he's screening my calls. "Hi, Jared, it's me," I say, turning a little so that Summer can't see my face. "I'm really sorry about what happened. Let me make it up to you, okay? Call me back."

I hang up, wondering if he'll even return the call. I decide to ask Jillian about this later, after she gets back from her married boyfriend's house.

Just then the phone rings and I swallow hard as I reach for it, thinking it's Jared. But the screen flashes an unfamiliar number. "Hello?" I call hopefully.

"Hi, Kim. It's Dena. How did your first day go?"

I glance at Summer sitting on the floor next to me, her eyes transfixed as Belle sang through the French countryside. First day? I've gotten into a fight with my boyfriend who's now drinking at another girl's house. I'm babysitting a kid who probably only likes me for my TV. And now I'm questioning if I'm even happy.

"Easy as pie," I say instead, because I will not have Dena feeling sorry for me.

"Really?" She lets out a relieved breath. "That's great!"

"Yeah," I say with false cheerfulness.

"Great," she says again, then pauses. "Listen, I wanted to give you a heads-up that I called a cleaning service. They'll be at your house tomorrow morning and will clean it top to bottom. Don't worry because I already paid for everything. Just answer the door when—"

"*What?*" I cry, not believing her. "You called a cleaning service?"

"Indeed, I did," Dena said. "I want Summer to be in a clean house. Is that so wrong? It's a free cleaning! Honestly," she begins, suddenly sounding indignant, "I thought you'd be more grateful..."

"Fine, fine." I roll my eyes, wondering what'd she do if I returned the favor.

"Come on, Kimmy. Don't be upset."

"It's fine," I say, then listen as she tells me the details of the cleaning service. When she's through, I yank the conversation to easier ground. "So, how's the vacation?"

"Oh, Kim," she says, sounding relieved to be changing topics. "It's just glorious here! The snow is so crisp and white and they have the most romantic bedroom suite I've ever seen. When Jonathan and I arrived, they had a bottle of Cristal waiting and a bed strewn with rose petals."

"Sounds great." I sigh.

"It is. Oh, I wish you were here..."

No, you don't. You want me stuck here so you can have the time of your life. You stay as far away as possible unless you want something from me.

I'm about to explode on the phone when Summer looks up at me and says, "Is that Mommy?"

I swallow the angry words and interrupt Dena, who's just explaining the hour-long massage she had with a gorgeous Italian. "Dena, Summer wants to talk to you."

"Oh! Great! Put her on."

I hand the phone to my niece and watch her face turn as bright as a halogen bulb. No matter how much Dena drives me crazy, she sure makes Summer happy.

I wonder if I can find that kind of happiness, too.

Chapter Five

SUNDAY, DECEMBER 11TH, 2005

"Mommy!"

I stretch against the dream. Sigh.

"*Mommy*!"

I groan and blink groggily as I squint into the neon green light of my digital clock. 2:58 A.M. "Oh my god," I whimper, tossing an arm over my throbbing eyes. "Please let it be a dream." I wait in the expectant silence for the cry I know will come.

"MOMMY!"

"All right!" I swing my legs out of bed and shove them into my purple bunny slippers. I shoulder my tattered robe and hobble into the living room, wincing as the strangled cry bleats through the cramped apartment.

Summer tosses amongst a barrage of pillows I'd assembled on the foldout couch and her face is sweaty and flushed. I rub my eyes as I sit next to her and reach out to stroke her wet forehead. "Summer," I say, squeezing her hand. "Babe, what is it?"

My niece's eyes glisten like caramel-colored marbles. Tears furrow down her pink cheeks. Guilt pangs through me like a gong.

Ugh. I'm a terrible aunt. Her first night here and she's already crying.

"Mommy," she whispers. "I want my Mommy."

I sigh and try to remain patient. "Your mother isn't here. You're staying with me for a while."

"But I want my Mommy."

"Yes," I strain, searching for the words that will calm my niece to sleep and allow me some of my own. "But you're with me now. You're just going to have to be a big girl and accept that. Can you be a big girl?"

Her lips quiver and her eyes threaten more tears, but she nods at length and squeezes my hand.

"Good," I say, lifting my chin with pride. "Now go to sleep and I'll see you in the morning, okay?"

I haven't taken two steps before I detect the tremor of a voice. "Can I sleep with you?"

When I turn around, Summer is gazing up at me hopefully. "Sleep with me? I, uh..."

"Please?" Her eyes are wide and pleading.

My defenses crumble. "Oh, all right."

Summer lets out a wild squeal and bounds from the couch along with a stuffed brown puppy in the protective crook of her arm. She gropes for my hand and marches beside me back to the bedroom, where she promptly executes a Superman leap onto the bed.

"Okay," I say, sliding under the coverlet and tucking a pillow under my ear. "Time for sleep."

The bed shakes as Summer settles into what seems like a thousand positions. After four minutes without a hint of peace, I groan, "Summer, please. Can you just sit still?"

"Tell me a story," she says as she props her chin against my waist.

"A story?" I glare at the clock. "Summer, it's three in the morning! We value sleep around here, you know."

"Then a quick one." She wiggles her head excitedly. "Please? *Please?*"

"Fine. Then will you promise to go to sleep?"

"Uh, huh."

I roll over and rack my brain for a story. Thirty seconds pass, but I'm still drawing a blank. "Okay," I begin, and Summer moves to settle against a pillow. "There once was a princess—"

"Was she pretty?"

"Uh, sure."

"What was her name?"

I give my niece a stern look. "How about Princess Kate?"

Summer shakes her head vehemently. "No, no. That's not a name for a princess!"

"It's not?"

"No," she says, then considers. "How about Princess Rebecca?" She attempts to roll the R, and it comes out garbled.

"Can't you roll your R's?" I ask her.

She shakes her head again. "Nope."

"Hasn't your mother tried to teach you?"

Summer looks surprised. "She knows how?"

"Of course," I say, remembering Dena was the only one who could speak what little Spanish the two of us knew without embarrassing herself.

"Oh. She never said."

I wonder why this is, but decide to let it pass. "Try this," I say, and then roll an R for a few seconds.

She follows my example, but her attempt sends spit flying.

We laugh. "No," I say, then think of how Mom used to teach others this technique. A memory tickles my mind. "Say 'pot of tea'."

"Pot of tea?" Summer queries.

"Yes. Pot of tea."

"Pot of tea."

"Faster."

"Pot of tea."

"Faster!"

"Pot of tea!"

"*Faster!*"

"Potoftea! Potoftea! *Para*tea!"

I clap excitedly. "Did you hear that? You rolled your R!"

Summer looks confused. "I did?"

"Sure. Say it again. Say *para ti*."

"*Para ti*," she says, suddenly hearing the roll of her R and letting out a jubilant cry.

"Terrific!" I say and spontaneously hug her. She's certainly a faster learner than I was at her age. "Great job."

"So what happens to Princess *Rrr*ebecca?" she asks, giggling.

I think for a moment. "So Princess *Rrr*ebecca lived in this castle with all of these servants and people waiting on her. Well, one day —"

"Did she have horses?" Summer cuts in.

"I don't know. I guess so."

"White or black ones?"

"Both."

"Any spotted ones?"

"A few. Whatever."

"Any unicorns?"

"Summer!" This could last hours if I'm not careful. Then I have an idea. "Why don't *you* tell the story?"

"Me?"

"Sure. Why not?"

"Okay," she says, then launches into a combination of Little Red Riding Hood, the Three Little Pigs, and Cinderella. She somehow threads the tales together and I can't help but be impressed. I envision her as an acclaimed novelist or Oscar-winning actress.

Twenty minutes later, Summer yawns and stretches her arms over her head. "That's how Mommy does it," she explains.

"What? Yawn?"

She nods.

I laugh. "And how does your dad do it?"

"Like this." Her mouth forms a wide O, and she stretches her arms up and to the sides, and then lowers a hand to scratch her small belly. We both erupt into laughter and for no discernible reason, I reach out and embrace my niece again. Summer squeezes me tightly and sighs contentedly against my shoulder.

I lean back and gaze at her, amazed at my sister's creation. I suddenly wonder if I'll ever have a daughter of my own.

Summer smiles and her teeth are as white as pearls. Then she pulls her stuffed puppy up to her chin and burrows deep under the covers.

I watch her fall into the rhythm of sleep and try to match her rapid breathing. *I could so keep a Chia Pet alive*, I think before surrendering to the welcoming darkness.

Chapter Six

Something warm stirs in my arms. I open my eyes to a pair of bright, shining orbs staring down at me.

"Morning, sleepyhead!" Summer exclaims, leaping from the bed and skirting out the door as if she'd been waiting hours for me to crack a single eyelid.

I roll over and pull the clock before my eyes. Five minutes until ten. At least the little bugger let me sleep in.

I yawn and throw my feet from the bed, mechanically slipping into my slippers and robe. Then I open the nightstand and sift through a few bills before my fingers graze the lid of a small worn box. I take it from the drawer and balance the weight between my fingers, opening it to reveal my mother's one-carat, brilliant-cut wedding ring.

Its facets catch the sunlight and sparkle like a mini disco ball. I gently take the ring from its black velvet enclosure and—as is my Sunday ritual—slip it onto my left ring finger and flex my hand before me.

I've done this every Sunday since the day I inherited my mother's ring. Every time I slide on the cool metal, I slip through space and time. Maybe it's silly, but I can almost sense her hand in mine.

I stand and plod down the hall to the bathroom, running my left hand along the short expense of the whitewashed wall. The ring's otherworldly comfort is worth more than its small weight of gold.

It's as the mint-flavored Crest suds are filling my mouth that it occurs to me that while Summer is thankfully potty trained (that is, after Dena arranged a small footstool by the toilet, which will probably lead to my eventual concussion) she probably hasn't brushed her teeth since the morning of her arrival. "Hey, Summer!" I call after spitting into the sink.

"What?" a voice returns from far away.

"Come here a sec!" I swish Listerine, then tip my head back to gargle.

"What'cha doing?" Summer asks, peeking sheepishly from behind the door. Her brown hair has spun into tight, electrocuted ringlets. She'd tucked the frilly hem of her nightgown into her panties. I can't suppress a grin.

"Brushing my teeth," I explain, blotting my mouth with a towel, "like you should be doing."

"No!" she exclaims, shaking her head defiantly.

"Oh, come on." I put on what I hope is a convincing smile. "It'll be fun. Where'd we put your bath stuff?"

Summer crosses her arms and says nothing as I comb through two suitcases. I finally find a plastic organizer suspended by a hanger that hooks conveniently behind the bathroom door. Dena also packed a choice of three toothpastes and I ask Summer which one she prefers.

She considers, staring up at the three small, multi-colored tubes. "Bubble gum," she says finally, as if it's killing her.

"Great." I unzip the pouch and remove the toothpaste and

corresponding brush. I squeeze a "pee-sized amount" onto the bristles as the instructions specify and hand it to her.

Summer then promptly sucks the toothpaste off the brush and swallows, grinning devilishly.

I watch this display with some amount of horror, wondering if I should contact Poison Control. But then Summer is laughing and I figure she's probably pulled this stunt before without lapsing into a coma. "All right," I say as I reapply the paste. "Let's try to do this like a big girl, okay?"

"Or...?" Summer counters with raised eyebrows.

I stare at her. "Or what?"

She waits a few moments. "Or else...?"

It takes a second to get where she's going with this. "Or else no dessert for a week." It's the best I can think of.

I've never been the best negotiator, but it seems to do the trick. I have never seen a child brush her teeth so fast and thoroughly. It's ironic how important dessert is in the priorities of a six-year-old, especially since society will eventually teach her to avoid it entirely.

While Summer is in the living room slurping Honey Nut Cheerios and re-engrossing herself in *Cinderella*, I think this is the perfect time to put on a pot of coffee and slip outside to get the Sunday paper.

It's as I'm opening the door that I run into three women, two of which are clutching buckets, rags, mops, and a vacuum. "Um, hello," I say, staring at them.

"Total Cleaning!" the oldest one announces. "We're here to clean your place. Are you Ms. Kincaid?"

"Yes," I say, and shake her hand.

"We heard you want us to focus on cigarette smoke, so we'll

tackle the carpets and furniture first. Is there anything else in partic-ular you would like us to focus on?"

I stare at them. I've never had my apartment cleaned before, and I guess it shows.

"Like yours curtains?" the woman prompts. "Fans? Baseboards?"

"Uh, that's fine." I think for a moment. "And I guess the bath-rooms?" They *were* pretty nasty. I wish I could get Jared to sit down when he pees, but he never even tries.

"You got it," the woman says with a curt nod. "Anything else?"

I shrug. "I guess just get it cleaned?"

They nod in unison and I step aside to let them pass.

I'm just bending down to pick up the yellow newspaper log when I hear a familiar voice say, "Good morning, Kim."

I adjust my glasses and tuck the paper under my arm. "Oh. Hi, Alice."

Alice Varady is the only other tenant close to my age who's not enrolled at the local university. She's a recent divorcée and has two young sons. We've only spoken twice and I otherwise wouldn't have remembered her name had I not caught her initials embossed on the breast pocket of her Terrycloth robe.

"I heard a child screaming in there last night," Alice says as she openly regards me. "Did you get pregnant, give birth, and miracu-lously lose all the weight, or are you babysitting?"

"The last one," I say as I take in Alice's casual bun of strawberry blonde hair, pressed cream-colored robe, and matching slippers. She's not what most would consider pretty, but even without a smear of mascara or lipstick, her face is radiant in that coveted natural way. "My sister's on vacation. She asked me to watch her kid."

"How old is she?"

I frown. "My sister?"

"No. Your niece."

"Oh!" I say, coloring with embarrassment. "Just turned six. I'm told she's not normally a banshee. She just misses her mom."

"That's completely normal. If you want, I—" But she's cut off as my newest patron scrambles behind me, proclaiming, "Aunt Kim! There's *people* here! And look! I dressed myself!" Her hair's a tangled nest, and she's wearing what appears to be a crushed purple velvet leotard beneath a frilly pink tutu, the latter of which I know I'd hidden away. I'm mortified for Alice to see my niece like this— because isn't it obvious whose fault it is?—but my neighbor hardly seems to notice.

Instead, Alice lowers herself to Summer's height and says, "Aren't you adorable?"

"Who are you?" Summer asks, clutching my legs.

"I'm Ms. Alice. What's your name?"

"Summer."

"Hello, Summer." She graciously extends a hand, which Summer tentatively accepts. "You're just adorable. But here, let me fix your pretty skirt." Alice adjusts the tutu and—after giving Summer an appraising look—pulls out her own hairband to style Summer's hair. Alice shoots me a smile and blows at the hair falling about her face.

Good grief. I would have never thought of that. My sister must have been tripping acid to grant me temporary custody.

Alice must read my thoughts, because she says, "You know, if you need any help, I'm just across the hall. It must be quite a shock to have a child take over your house."

"No shit," I say, watching as my niece performs ballet in my kitchen.

"No *shoot*," Alice corrects.

"What?"

"No *shoot*. You'll have to watch your language around kids. They pick it up like a virus."

"Oh," I reply, embarrassed as a stricken teenager.

"Don't worry about it," Alice says, and then leans in as if to tell me a secret. "Once I stubbed my toe and accidentally said 'fuck.' My oldest son heard, and it took me a week to convince him I'd said *fudge*." We laugh and after a moment she asks, "So what do you two have planned for the day?"

I shrug. "Not a clue. But we have to do something because my sister is having my house cleaned."

Alice whistles. "That's so nice of her!"

"Yeah, I guess so," I say, suddenly hearing a vacuum turn on in the distance.

"You'll want to be out of your place for sure. I'm taking Dillon and Troy to the park in about a half-hour. Do you want to join us?"

I consider this. The only time I've been to a park was to make out with my first boyfriend. "I don't know…"

"Come on. It'll be fun. What have you got to lose?"

I gradually relent. "What do you do there?"

"All sorts of things. The boys like to play Frisbee or catch. I read or take a walk. It's really relaxing."

"Oh." In truth, it sounds boring as hell, but I've nothing better planned and figure she's right. What have I got to lose? Plus, it would be good to be with an adult, at least until Jared gets home. "Okay," I say. "That sounds like fun."

"Great." Alice turns to go. "By the way, congratulations."

"Excuse me?"

Her gaze pointedly lowers to my mother's wedding ring.

"Oh!" I instantly slip the offending hand behind my back. "No, no. I'm not engaged."

"But…"

"I know what it looks like," I stammer, starting to sweat. "It's…

uh...it's not even real. I just wear it so guys at work don't hit on me. I guess it got stuck."

"Oh," she says curiously. "Well, okay, then. So I'll come by in a half-hour. Think you can be ready?"

"No problem," I say, already wrestling off the ring and wondering how I'm going to get Summer out of that tutu without enduring World War III.

The knock at my door comes exactly twenty-nine minutes later, and I scramble across the living room to answer it.

Alice stands smiling at me, looking as put-together as someone on the cover of Working Mother magazine. She wears a creamy turtle-neck with a pair of jeans and sneakers and small gold hoop earrings with a matching bracelet and watch. A yellow and white checkered bag fits over her right shoulder, a black coat folds into the crook of her arm, and flanking her slim thighs are her two sons with matching green fleeces and black pants, staring up at me in quiet obedience.

"Dillon, Troy," she says in a soft, motherly cadence. "You remember Ms. Kincaid, don't you?"

"Hello," they reply in unison. They look like cherubs.

"Hi," I say, then call over my shoulder, "Summer! Can you get over here? We're ready to go."

Nothing. I call again. Silence. "I'll be right back," I say, leaving the door ajar as I go in search of my niece. One cleaner points to the bedroom, where I find her sitting cross-legged on the carpet. "What are you doing?"

She doesn't immediately meet my eyes. "I don't want to go."

"Oh, come on, Summer. It'll be fun. You were looking forward to it a little while ago."

"I changed my mind."

I hold my hand out towards her. "Come on, honey. Everybody's waiting."

She whispers something under her breath.

"What did you say?"

"They're going to make fun of me."

"What? That's crazy! Why do you think they'll make fun of you?"

"I look like a baby," she says, pulling at her neon-green cotton pants and matching long-sleeved shirt. I'd slipped a pair of Nikes over her feet and pulled her hair into pigtails, curling each tendril so that she looked like Shirley Temple. I think she looks rather stylish. Certainly more than I do, anyway. For once, I'd opted out of my spiky heels, instead choosing dusty jogging sneakers and sweatpants. I'd even skipped the makeup, having only just enough time for two swipes of lip gloss. I can only hope that male passersby don't immediately avert their eyes in disgust.

"You don't look like a baby," I tell her firmly. "You look like a nice young lady."

Summer remains unconvinced. "No, I don't."

"You do too," I say, beckoning her with my outstretched hand. "Come on now. You don't look like a baby, but you're beginning to *act* like one."

Summer blinks and then shifts her gaze to my hand. With a *huff*, she slips her hand into mine and allows herself to be pulled to her feet.

"That's better," I say, adjusting Summer's top and scrunching her pigtails with a few quick pulses of my hand. I grab her Burberry coat and zip it up to her chin. "You look great."

I snatch my jacket as we walk out together. "Crisis averted," I say, calmly triumphant.

"What a cute outfit you're wearing, Summer," Alice gushes. "You look beautiful."

Summer says nothing and I shoot her a pointed look. "What do you say, Summer?"

"Thank you," she mumbles without looking up.

Alice smiles. "So how old are you, Summer?"

"Six." Barely a whisper.

"Six? That's amazing! What a big girl you are. You know, my boys aren't that much older than you." She turns to introduce her sons. "Summer, this is Dillon and Troy. Dillon is seven and Troy is your age. Boys, this is Summer."

"Hello," the eldest—Dillon—says, smiling at her. I notice he has perfect white teeth and will probably never need braces. His curly blonde hair is just like his mother's, brushed neatly into place. I wonder how the hell Alice does it.

"Hi," Troy says. He still has most of his baby fat and has beautiful blue eyes and straight, chestnut-colored hair.

Summer stares at the two of them before issuing a nearly inaudible, "Hello."

"And we're off!" I announce, shooing Summer out the door.

Alice gives me a quick glance and casually asks, "Did you remember to bring any toys or snacks?"

"Snacks?" I echo. "For what?"

"In case Summer gets hungry." She looks at me expectantly.

"Oh. No, I forgot. Hold on..." I'm already reaching for the door.

"Don't worry about it." Alice pats her checkered bag. "I've got plenty to share."

I nod in relief. The five of us start down the hall. Once Summer's hand slips into mine, I whisper to Alice, "Thank you."

She shoots me a wry grin. "I wouldn't say that yet. The day's only just begun."

❄

The sun is bright and high in the sky, warming the westerly wind that blows gently on our exposed hands and faces. Summer's mood has markedly improved. She catches up with Dillon and Troy and they bookend either side of her slender frame, looking like something out of *The Wizard of Oz* as they stroll down the path toward their collective destiny.

I sneak quick glances at Alice, who is walking beside me humming "Tell Him". I can't get over how *together* she is. We're practically the same age, but Alice has been married, delivered two children, lives in an apartment twice the size of mine, and has a job that pays enough for her knock-off designer clothes and regular manicures.

"So what do you do?" I ask abruptly.

She glances at me and smiles. "I'm a registered nurse."

"Wow." We walk a few steps in silence. "So, do you like your job?"

She gives a noncommittal shrug. "It's okay. I only work three days a week, but each day has a fourteen-hour shift. I wanted to be a doctor, you know."

"Really?" I wonder what stopped her.

"Yeah. But you know. Things happen." She shrugs again. "You're probably wondering why I'm living in an apartment and not a real house."

"No, I'm not," I lie.

She gives a mirthless laugh. "Well, I can tell you, what you see isn't necessarily the entire picture. The divorce…" Her voice trails into silence.

"What?"

She shakes her head, and her bright eyes suddenly cloud. "I was just thinking about Eric."

"Your husband?" I assume. "I mean ex?"

"The one and only."

"Why did you get divorced?" I ask, unable to help myself. "Sorry, I didn't mean to pry. You don't have to answer that."

"It's okay. There were a lot of contributing factors. But I'd say the forerunner was the fact that he cheated on me."

I come to a dead stop. "No way!"

She turns towards me. "Is it that shocking?"

"Yes! I mean, you're so nice and smart and..."

"It's not always about that," Alice says, starting us up again. She gazes ahead at her sons with great affection. "I really wanted a family and pushed him for it. We'd already been married for five years, and I didn't want to wait forever. So I stopped taking my birth control, and it wasn't too long before I was pregnant with Dillon."

"Wow," I say, admiring her ability to charge after her future.

"Well, you can't change a man. He wasn't ready before and he certainly wasn't ready for the responsibility afterward." She pauses. "Are you sure you want to hear about all this?"

"Only if you want to talk about it."

She runs a hand through her hair. "Actually, it sort of helps, talking about it. When I had Dillon, I practically raised him myself. I wanted another child, but Eric was dead-set against it. I stopped taking the Pill and soon we had Troy."

"And he wasn't ready for that either."

"No," she says, her face clouding further. "He hated the responsibility that came with children. The problem was we were so different. Having children made him feel old, whereas I feel even more alive." She sighs and looks away. "I guess I got what I deserved."

I instinctively put my hand on her arm.

"I'm sorry," she corrects. "I don't mean to say that I deserved it. Only that his reaction was not unexpected. Another woman gave him a shot of youth and freedom. I just wasn't making him feel that way anymore."

"Bastard."

She smiles. "My sentiments exactly."

"What did you do when you found out?"

"Oh, it was awful. I spent the first two months trying to figure out what to do. My parents are still married and I wanted that stability for my sons. But Eric and I argued all the time. Even though he promised not to see the other woman again, I still felt he wasn't spending enough time with the boys and me. And he wasn't happy." She sighs. "I finally realized that their father and I were so different that being raised in our house would probably be worse than living apart."

"You're so brave," I say, imagining what it would take to end a marriage and raise two young children. Then I realize that my mother did exactly that, after our dad died.

"Anyway," Alice continues, "I'm saving for a house and hopefully we can move out soon. An apartment just isn't the proper place to raise children."

I shrug. "I wouldn't know."

There's a long silence. Eventually Alice shakes her head as if to clear it, then turns to look at me. "So I've seen you with a very cute man. Is he your boyfriend?"

I puff up like a rooster. "Yes, he is. His name's Jared."

"How long have you been seeing him?"

"A little over two years."

"Not bad. Do you love him?"

I hesitate before nodding resolutely. "Yes."

"And does he feel the same way?"

"I think so." I quickly add, "He's not said it, but I know he must. We've been together for so long that he probably figures it doesn't need to be said."

"Oh."

I see her glancing at me in my peripheral vision and I know she's wondering why he still hasn't said he loves me, that she finds the omission strange. Why can't Jared just admit the truth? What's wrong with him, anyway? What's wrong with me?

"So," she says after a pause. "How do you see your future turning out?"

"I hope to get married."

"To Jared?"

"Of course. Who else?"

I think she senses that this is making me uncomfortable, because she says, "So what do you do, Kim?"

I wish I could say something fabulous, like a doctor, professor, or corporate CEO. Something that would guarantee a lifetime of security and happiness like it has for my sister. I've been everything from a waitress to a lingerie specialist, but at least now I have a job that covers health insurance. "I'm a legal secretary," I say at last.

"That's nice." Alice smiles encouragingly. "For whom?"

"The university."

"Wow. That sounds interesting."

"It's really not."

There's a pause. "Well, they must keep you pretty busy."

"It's actually really boring," I admit. "I just wish—"

I'm cut off as Summer bounds towards me, clutching something in her hand. "Aunt Kim!" she cries. "Aunt Kim!"

"Yes?" I say, lowering myself to her level.

"Look what I found!" She reveals an enormous brown pinecone.

"That's nice," I say, for lack of anything better.

"You know," Alice says, touching the pinecone with her right index finger, "we can paint it and sprinkle some glitter on it and turn it into an ornament."

"Whoa!" Summer says, turning it over in her hand as if imagining it suspended from the bough of a Christmas tree. "Can we really do that?"

"Of course," Alice says.

"Sounds great," I say, wondering why I hadn't thought of it first.

"Thanks, Aunt Kim!" Summer exclaims, rushing to give me a kiss.

My mood instantly brightens. I smile down at her. "No problem, kiddo."

Summer dashes ahead to intercept the boys who are busy playing Frisbee. Alice motions to a bench and we take a seat. "So, how are you in the grocery department?"

"Not that great." I recite most of the contents in my pantry and whatever I can remember from my freezer and fridge. Alice nods.

"I'd get a bunch of snacks and easy-to-cook meals," she suggests and then adds with a wink, "and—as a personal recommendation—a bottle of Advil."

Alice leaves a scribbled list of items she thinks I need and sends me to the grocery store with her shopper's discount card. I ask if she wants to come along, but she has to drop her sons off with their father, which, she explains, "Is a job in itself."

After a heated debate in which Summer demands to push the cart—a physically impossible feat, considering her hands don't even reach the handlebar—she finally settles on sitting inside the cart, which I wisely dub, "The Throne."

We wander up and down the aisles together and I deeply enjoy the occasional, "What a pretty girl!" or "Your daughter is adorable!" from shoppers without bothering to correct them.

Just as we're halfway through the baking aisle, Summer gyrates wildly, flinging her arms out in what I predict will be a nasty tantrum. "I want out!" she cries. "*I* want to push the cart!"

"No," I say firmly, reddening as an older woman passes us and shakes her head disapprovingly. I know she's thinking she can do better, that *she* would have her child under control.

"I want out!" Summer howls, waving her arms. "*Now!*"

"NO!" I shout, startling both of us with my outburst. Summer's bottom lip trembles and I heave a sigh. Seconds later she is a tempest of tears and in three minutes I'm swimming through a series of threats, negotiations, pleas, and deals with the Devil.

Suddenly Summer heaves her arms out of the cart and accidentally topples a magazine stand. The crash of metal on linoleum jars us both, and for a moment the storm abates. "Now look what you've done," I say through clenched teeth, bending down to collect the scattered contents.

Her sobs thankfully subside. "I'm s—sorry," she stammers.

"You should be." She's still tearful, so I try to soften my voice. "It's okay. It's fine."

She sniffs and slowly nods.

I fix the metal rack and start shoving the magazines into random slots. The last bunch on the floor catches my eye as I pick them up.

One magazine showcases an attractive thirtyish woman dressed in a beige suit, her honey-colored hair in soft curls with only a hint of makeup on her face. Comparatively, my wardrobe, accessories, and makeup looked gaudy and cheap.

"What's wrong?" Summer calls from the cart.

I glance at my niece and smile tightly. "Nothing, sweetie," I say, tossing the copies into a random shelf and push the cart up the aisle. "Nothing at all."

My cell erupts with a ring. I fish through my purse and bring it to my ear. "Hello?"

"Where *are* you?" Jillian demands.

"What do you mean?"

"I mean, we were supposed to meet for coffee. I've been at Barnes and Noble for fifteen minutes, waiting for you."

I wince. "Oh my god. I'm sorry, Jillian. I've been busy."

"Excuses, excuses!" she scoffs. "Just tell me you're on your way and I'm not being stood up after all."

"I'm on my way," I sigh, then hang up and say to Summer, "Come on, kiddo. Duty calls."

Chapter Seven

THURSDAY, SEPTEMBER 2, 2004

Oh, dear God. Oh, sweet Jesus.

I'm sitting in the driver's seat with my heart hammering in my ears. I have just skimmed my Prism into the back of someone's Accord. The Honda's right taillight had given a hideous crack, and now glass peppers the asphalt. I check my rearview mirror. I am alone in this aisle of the Wal-Mart parking lot—a rarity. So far as I can tell, no one has seen me hit this car.

The back of my neck goes hot. I seriously cannot afford the higher insurance premium that is sure to come.

I check the mirror again. Still alone.

I could simply back up and drive away. I could just leave. No one would ever know.

Guilt spreads the more I think about it. I remember the time I discovered a dent on the side of my car. I'd wanted to kill the bastard that had left the mark and ran. I can't do this to someone, even if it is a stranger.

So I park a few spaces away from the car and wait, the sweat pouring down the sides of my face and my stomach twisting into nervous knots. I imagine some linebacker coming out in a fury, threatening to beat up the perpetrator. Then I imagine a popular, cheerleader-type with a throng of friends who will stomp my self-esteem into pieces.

Eventually, a petite, thirtyish woman in a tan trench coat and a short bob strides towards the Honda with a cart in front of her. She stops when she sees the rear. I can't hear what she says, but I suspect she's swearing.

I get out of my car and slowly walk towards her. "Hi," I say, my voice strangely thick.

But she doesn't hear me. "Jesus. I can't *believe* this! What a fucked-up day this has turned out to be!"

"Excuse me," I say, tapping her shoulder.

She turns and gives me an angry glance.

"Listen, I'm really sorry, but I'm the one who hit your car."

There's a pause, and her eyes narrow slightly. "*You* hit my car?"

Sweat beads across my forehead. "Yes. I'm really sorry. I just..."

"Wait," she says, putting up a hand. "*You* hit my car?"

Oh my god. She's really pissed. "Yes. Again, I'm really sorry—"

"And you've been waiting outside to tell me this?"

"Uh, yes. I didn't want to just run off and not own up to this. It's a pretty rotten thing to happen. I know, because it's happened to me."

The woman gives me a full look-over. Then—to my complete shock—she breaks into a wide grin. She puts out her hand. "Jillian," she says. "Jillian Martin."

"Oh," I say, taking her hand. "I'm Kim Kincaid. Again, I'm really..."

"It's fine," she says, waving her hand. "You got coverage?"

"Yes," I say, instinctively turning to retrieve my insurance card.

She stops me. "It's okay for now. What are you up to?"

I blink for a moment in confusion. "Up to?"

"Yeah. What were you going to do before you hit my car?"

"I was about to go grocery shopping."

"Forget that. Feel like grabbing a drink? I've had the shittiest day and need someone to whine to about it."

"O—okay," I say, smiling with both surprise and relief. She's really nice, considering the circumstances. And I owe her a drink, at the very least.

Within an hour, we're gossiping over chardonnay and telling stories of failed romances. Jillian is so easy to talk to that I cannot believe what I tell her—it just spills from my mouth.

"You're Puerto Rican? Like, *Hispanic*?" she says, looking at me like I'm from Mars. "I would have never known from looking at you."

Already I regret telling her. "Well, it's not like we're a different species." Then I pause. "You wouldn't have known just by looking at me? Truly? My whole life, people have—" But I stop before I embarrass myself further. She doesn't need to know everything I went through. I don't want her pitying me.

"No, I'm sorry," she says, placing her hand on mine. "I didn't mean what that sounded like. I mean—shit, I don't know what I mean. It's cool, though, that you're *Latina*." She says this last part with a funny lilt and I laugh.

"Really? Why?"

"Well, the Jennifer Lopez thing is making it very cool to be Hispanic. And Julio Iglesias. And Ricky Martin. And..." She searches for words. "Ricky Ricardo?"

"From *I Love Lucy*? That's the best you can think of?"

She giggles. "Sorry. But I think it's neat that you have ethnic roots. I don't have a unique bone in my body. Completely English and German. My people were the oppressors."

"Mine raped and pillaged."

She gives me a strange look. "The Puerto Ricans?"

"No, the Spanish," I clarify, laughing with her. "That's where my mother and father's grandparents were from, originally."

"So, both of your parents are Puerto Rican?"

"Only my Mom was fully Puerto Rican. My Dad was half."

"That's so neat! So they speak Spanish and everything?"

I redden. "Well, they did. They died a while back."

"Oh." Jillian's smile evaporates. "I'm sorry."

My blush deepens. Clearly, I'd overshared. "It was a while ago."

Jillian gives a slow, thoughtful nod. "So, was that your only family?"

"No. I have a sister, Dena. But we're not that close."

She frowns. "Sorry again."

I wave my hand at her, dismissing her sentiments. "Don't worry. I've come to terms with everything. Really."

"Well, okay." Jillian clears her throat and then raises her glass in a toast. "To fresh starts?"

"Fresh starts," I agree, clinking my glass with hers.

"Well, if it helps," Jillian offers at length, "I have a sister too, and we're not close at all. What I lack in familial relationships, I make up in girlfriends. *¿Comprendano?*"

"*Sí,*" I agree, grinning at her terrible Spanish.

"Good, because that's the only word I know."

And for the first time, I'm laughing with someone about my heritage, instead of being laughed at. It's an amazing feeling—one I've not felt in a long, long time. Maybe it's that and the cheap wine that emboldens me to say, "Do you think we could be friends?"

Jillian smiles as she says, "Aren't we already?"

Chapter Eight

"But I thought you were taking care of her *next* weekend," Jillian says, eyeing Summer, who's at the adjacent table absorbed with a stack of children's books and a small cup of hot chocolate.

"You know I've never been good at remembering dates."

"Yeah. I know." She gingerly sips her cappuccino. "So how's it going?"

"It's not easy," I admit. "I'm still getting used to it."

"Hmmm." She looks at Summer again, then turns her excited eyes back to me. "Okay. So my boss—"

"Who you're having an affair with," I put in with a purposely judgmental raise of one eyebrow.

"Come on, Kim. His wife doesn't understand him."

I have to laugh at this. "That's such a cliché, Jillian. All married men claim the same thing."

She rolls her eyes as if this is irrelevant. "It still doesn't change the fact that she's horrible to him. Do you know that when she calls the office, and he's busy, she tells us—his *employees*—what a horrible husband and even worse father he is?"

"Geez. He has kids too?"

"Kim!" Her navy blazer creases as she folds her arms across her chest. "Come on already. You're not making this easy for me."

I take a breath and settle back into the booth, taking a long, contemplative sip of my mochachino.

"Do you hate me?" she asks, and her voice is different. Small.

I look at her as if she is kidding, but realize that she is serious. "Of course I don't hate you. I hate the situation, but not you."

She nods with relief. "Thanks."

"So, how did this whole thing start?" She has yet to disclose any major details, so I suspect her sudden need to meet over coffee is just for that.

Jillian smiles, then delicately unties her cashmere scarf and folds it over her wool coat that's hanging behind her chair. While I can only gaze through store windows at such articles, Jillian parades them because she's the chief assistant to Adam Bell of Weinstein and York law offices. She gets Christmas bonuses and three workdays off a month, makes upwards of seventy thousand, owns a fabulous twenty-five hundred square foot condo in the suburbs and a brand-new Honda. Yet one would guess that while I make less than a third of her salary, I still have more in savings since she spends her paychecks on needless expenditures. But then I shouldn't criticize since she is the one who helped me find my current job, even if it is boring as hell and I'm forced to sit three feet away from Evil Incarnate.

"I guess it started when Adam transferred to our offices a few months ago," she begins, blushing as if relieving the experience. "He kept me on even after my previous boss quit, and the day we met, I felt an immediate spark between us. It was practically *electric*. For the first two months, he'd chat me up before and after work. Just harmless flirting, really. We just had so much in common..." She pauses. "Except, of course, for him being married. I started really looking forward to seeing him, dressing better than I could afford. Anyway, eventually I caught him checking me out and I *knew*."

There's a beat. "Knew what?"

"That he liked me." A knowing smile plays on her lips as she twirls a strand of hair around her index finger. "And that I liked him, too."

I nod, wanting so much for my friend to be happy, but sad it should come at the cost of another woman's marriage.

"And then two weeks ago, I was staying late at the office working on a brief and he came to my desk to hand me some more pages. When he leaned in to see my monitor, he put his hand on my back. Then..." She sighs. "I swear, Kim. He smelled—*smells*—glorious. Something dark and primal."

"Oh please," I cut in. "This is hardly Harlequin."

She waves a hand. "Whatever. So when we kissed..." She pauses dramatically. "*Fireworks*. And in bed..." She sighs. "The best of my *life*."

I manage a tepid smile. It's obvious that Jillian's happy, but something like this won't end well. I glance over at Summer, still captivated by her picture books.

Jillian stops twirling her hair and leans forward. "I just don't know what to do from here, though. You have to help me."

This catches me a little off guard. "Help you how?"

Her hands reach across the table to grasp mine. "I think I'm falling in love with him."

I shake my head. "Oh no. No, no, *no*."

"Please help me."

"Why? What do you want me to do?"

"I need you to meet his wife."

"What!" I snatch my hands back.

"I just want to know what I'm up against. Is she pretty? Smart? Interesting? Or—shudder—all the above?"

"You haven't met her yet?"

"No. She just calls the office. But I think she suspects something."

"Good Lord. Why?"

"When she calls and I say he's in a meeting, she makes a point to talk to me."

My shoulders relax. "That doesn't sound so bad."

"But you don't know the questions she asks."

"Like...?"

"Am I married? Do I have kids? Do I have a boyfriend? Am I seeing anyone special?"

"Really? She asks you all that?"

"God yes."

I finish my drink and return the empty cup to its saucer. "Sounds like she knows something's up. So what's your boss have to say about all this?"

Jillian lets out a dejected sigh. "That's just it. *Nothing*. I have a feeling he just wants to keep things the way they are."

What man wouldn't? I think, but keep my gaze neutral. "So, what are you going to do?"

"I don't know. Keep trying? I figure his feelings will come around. Eventually."

"Oh, Jillian."

"What?"

"Just don't put your whole heart in this. You don't know his true intentions."

"His intentions are *me*," she says assuredly.

Suddenly there's a crash on our left and I turn to see Summer's hot chocolate running all over the stack of children's books. "Uh oh!" Summer cries, looking horrified.

"Oh, *man!*" I snatch all of our napkins and quickly rush to soak up the hot liquid. "Summer!"

"I'm sorry! I'm sorry!" Her eyes brim with tears.

"I'll get more napkins," Jillian says and runs off.

"What happened?" I demand, seeing the pages of every book curl and discolor.

"I dunno. I was just reading, and it tipped itself over."

"I'm sure," I mumble, just as Jillian returns with two handfuls of napkins.

"Ma'am!" calls a sharp voice.

I turn to meet the disapproving gaze of a book clerk. "Yes?" I say, frantically dabbing at the pages.

"You're going to have to pay for those."

"Really?" I gaze dejectedly at the six hardcover books I'd plucked randomly from the shelves. "But if I just—"

"*Now*," she says, picking them up in her hands and marching to the checkout counter.

"What a bitch," Jillian murmurs to me.

I glare at Summer, who follows us like a beaten dog to the register. "I'm sorry, Aunt Kim," she says miserably.

My anger fades until the computer spits out a bill of $73.50. "But they're children's books!" I protest.

The clerk is unforgiving. "Credit, check, or cash?"

"I am *so* getting my tubes tied," Jillian murmurs as she thumbs through a magazine.

I glare at her. "Jillian! My niece is right here!"

"Oh, like she knows what that means!"

I glumly hand over my credit card. After the clerk passes me the ruined books in a plastic bag, Jillian asks, "So. Are you headed home?"

"I probably should," I say, not wanting to chance Summer destroying anything else.

Jillian and I slip on our coats, and I bend to help Summer into hers. As the three of us push through the doors into the December cold, Jillian says, "So how's work?"

"Not great." I sigh. "They rag me for coming in late from lunch. I swear, an extra five minutes and bam! I'm an awful employee."

"My boss doesn't care if I'm ten, even twenty minutes late after lunch."

I give her a look and whisper, "That's because you're sleeping with him."

She beams. "I know! So what about spying on Adam's wife? Can you do it?"

"Heck, no."

"Please?"

"I said no, you crazy woman. You're on your own in this."

"Fine. You wait until you need a favor and this will come back to haunt you."

"We'll see." I give her a quick kiss on the cheek before waving goodbye.

"What was she talking about?" Summer asks as I buckle her into the booster seat.

I grin at her. "I have no idea. That woman is as crazy as a bat."

She giggles. "Bats aren't crazy!"

"Then what is?"

She considers. "Mommy, sometimes. When I don't wipe my shoes."

I laugh. "Now *that* is crazy."

I retract the words the moment I open the door. My apartment's clean from top to bottom, the plush carpet faintly tracked from a vacuum. The couch is scented with flowers. The sink, counters, table, and chairs are all polished to a high shine—even the usually dusty screen of the television.

I check the bathroom, where fresh towels fold over the bars. The toilet paper's outermost ply is bent into an artful triangle.

Lordy. Is this what Dena comes home to every day? No wonder she freaks if Summer drags in mud from the backyard!

The cleaning women are just finishing up. I thank them almost to the point of embarrassment. But, honestly. My place has never looked so good.

The feeling doesn't last. A minute after they leave, my elation fades into bitterness.

Once again, Dena had saved the day.

And once again, I'm in her debt.

Chapter Nine

MONDAY, DECEMBER 12TH, 2005

At 6:35 on Monday morning, I'm dressed and squatting beside Summer, straightening a pair of stockings beneath a red skirt and long-sleeved cotton shirt. I'm rarely up this early—I don't have to be at work until eight-thirty—but I want to make sure Summer's ready for daycare on time.

As I struggle with her clothes, Summer stands above me with her hands on my shoulders, staring off into the distance.

"Are you excited?" I ask, grimacing as I try to smooth a persistent wrinkle from the stocking.

"No," she says.

"You're not excited to go to Ben & Jerri's?" I'm excited to see it, imagining ice cream counters and vats of chocolate sauce. It had to be a cool place with a name like that!

"Not really."

"Well, it should be fun. They probably have tons of games."

"Uh, huh."

"There!" I stand up to survey her. "Perfect."

I've combed Summer's hair into a ponytail and secured an enormous frilly white bow at the top of her head. She looks adorable.

But Summer says nothing, only looks at me with wide, pleading eyes. "Can't I just stay with you?"

"No, honey. I've got to go to work." I bend down and embrace her small, resisting body. "You understand, don't you?"

"Yes." She turns and walks away, then says just loud enough for me to hear, "Just like Mommy and Daddy."

Summer's hand is cold and clammy in mine as the two of us walk down the pastel green hallway to the front desk of Ben & Jerri's. An obese, platinum blonde woman sits behind the counter, reading a Harlequin romance novel. She is so engrossed that she doesn't even notice us until I speak up.

"Hello," I say, ignoring Summer, who is repeatedly tugging at my hand. She is trying to guilt me into not leaving her. *Which is just what I'm doing,* I think miserably. *Leaving her.*

"Ah, yes," the woman says, discreetly tucking the book under a stack of papers. "How can I help you?"

"My name's Kim Kincaid, and I'm here with my niece, Summer. My sister arranged for her to stay here over the next two weeks."

"Last name?"

"Nordstrom. Summer Nordstrom."

"Nordstrom?" she says, her eyes brightening. "Any relation to the store?"

"Nope," I say, well used to this question. "Pure coincidence."

"Oh," she says, deflating a little. "Okay, then. Nordstrom..." She licks a thick finger and thumbs through a few pages in a folder. "Ah, yes. Here we are. That's fine then." She abruptly turns and calls through a small window behind her desk, "Bethany! Hey, *Bethany*!"

A moment later, a door opens at the end of the hall and a young woman with plaited brown hair strides towards us.

The woman at the desk says, "Looks like we've got a recruit."

Bethany smiles brightly and says, "We do, do we?" She squats next to Summer and says, "And what's your name, little Miss?"

Summer stares back at her and says nothing.

"Come on, honey," I implore. "Tell the nice lady your name."

Summer gazes up at me with watery eyes. "Please, just take me home. *Please.*"

Before I can respond, Bethany tut-tuts and says, "We get a lot of this, Ma'am. But don't worry. She'll be safe and sound with us." She reaches for Summer's hand, but the girl recoils. "Oh, come on, sweetie," she says soothingly. "You're okay."

Summer's bottom lip quivers and I instinctively embrace her. "It's okay," I say, stroking her hair. "I'll be here to pick you up right at five-thirty. Not a minute later."

Her voice is a shaky whisper. "*Please* don't leave me here."

"It's fine," Bethany assures. She reaches for Summer's arm and gives it a careful tug.

At that moment, Summer bursts into tears and reaches for me. "Don't leave me, Aunt Kim!"

Hot tears push at the back of my eyes. But I know I must stand firm. "I'll be back at five-thirty. Not a minute later."

Bethany smiles encouragingly and picks her up. "Nooooo..." Summer howls down the hall, reaching with both hands over Bethany's shoulder. "Come back..."

"It's okay, Ms. Kincaid," says the lady behind the counter. "We're used to this at drop off. Especially the first time."

I nod numbly as the double doors at the end of the hall swing shut and the wails fade into silence. I swallow hard and drag myself to my car, where I promptly collapse into tears.

I push through the office's double glass doors and stagger to the far corner, where a set of gray filing cabinets flank my tiny cubicle.

"You're late," Lisa calls after me.

I avoid her eyes. "Sorry."

"Lord, what happened to you? You look like hell." There's a pause, and then Lisa's eyes widen with knowing. "Oh my god."

I glance at her. "What?"

"Did you and Jared break up?"

"No." I scowl as I arrange myself at my desk. "Why would you say that?"

She quickly recovers. "It just looks like you've been crying."

"Well, it's not because of that, I can assure you." I smooth down my hair, wondering why I had balled like that in the car. *Must be pre-menstrual.* "I'm babysitting my niece for the next few weeks. I had to drop her off at daycare and it sort of got to me."

Lisa gives a distracted nod. "Well, you better watch out. They're noticing your tardiness."

Only because you tell them, I think.

"Well?" she says, looking haughty.

"Sorry," I say, wondering why I'm always apologizing. She's not my boss—at least not technically. It's difficult to define the parameters of our relationship. Lisa is the administrative assistant to Paul Mitchell, a university lawyer who flits in and out of the office and always looks worried and sleep-deprived. My boss is Larry Thompson, Paul's subordinate. I answer to both Paul and Larry, and even to Lisa, if there are witnesses. Lisa only answers to Paul, and even then she's known for passing his assignments over to me. She's worked for the university over six years—five longer than I have—and so by rights has seniority. I tread carefully around Lisa because I know her influence could have me fired.

"Nice sweater," she says eventually.

"Oh. Thanks." But Lisa laughs and I realize she's joking. She thinks my reindeer sweater is hideous.

I glance at Lisa as she smiles a commercial-worthy grin. I wish I looked good in red lipstick. Instead, I'm relegated to the dark browns that make my teeth look whiter (the trick of a smoker who can't afford to bleach). Jillian rages against my robin-egg blue eye shadow, but I think it opens my tired eyes and makes me pretty—or at least marginally so.

"You're late," says Larry—my actual boss—as he strides out of his office.

I try to cover my embarrassment with a smile. "Sorry. It won't happen again." In this job, I do a lot of apologizing.

But why does it even matter? My sole task is to digitally catalogue and cross-reference every one of our files from 1957 to the present. Our office alone has sixty-seven drawers with about three hundred files each, not to mention the dungeon of files we keep in storage downstairs. Why Larry decided this was a priority is beyond me. I've slogged through about twenty drawers, knowing that I could have conquered nearly double that had it not been for the Internet and the careful repositioning of my flat panel. I probably spend four of my nine hours here cataloging, an hour—perhaps two —editing legal agreements and filing garnishments (Lisa's job) and the rest writing e-mails to Jillian, surfing the web, and ranking expert at Solitaire. I can do all this because nobody really takes notice of me unless I'm gone. This is one of the few instances in my life where being nondescript actually works to my benefit.

"I'm stepping out for a break," Lisa says after Larry closes his door. She flashes a fake smile as she picks up her jacket and takes off. I think she hates me, but Jillian says I'm being ridiculous because someone that shallow cannot possibly harbor genuine emotions.

Neither Paul nor Larry seems to care that Lisa takes a "break" five hours during the week—not counting the hour-long lunch each day (they barely let me escape for the seven minutes of a cigarette). If her chair's empty, they simply pass her work over to me, making me wonder why the hell Lisa makes six thousand more a year than I do.

I suspect the only reason I still have my job is that I have a mind for math and know how to stay organized (despite my apartment). This office was a wreck when I first arrived, with files strewn over counters and stacked in corners, desks and floors cluttered with heaps of wiring, the shredder overflowing and walking paths obstructed. Armed with two cans of Endust, multiple rags, and eleven storage boxes, I spent every spare moment reorganizing. I filed every loose item, spooled the cables, stocked the shelves and even added a faux rhododendron. Just last week, I pasted plastic snowflakes onto the glass doors and plugged in a set of colored Christmas lights, all discovered in the back of an overhead cabinet, untouched for a decade.

I flinch as the door opens. A pretty woman in an ivory blazer and matching camisole strides in with a smaller woman in tow.

"Can I help you?" I ask, rising from my chair.

As the woman rummages through her chocolate and cream Gucci purse, she brushes her hair with her left hand, showing off an enormous canary diamond wedding ring. She doesn't even look at me when she says, "I'm a friend of Paul's, here to see him."

"Okay," I say, walking to her. I'm about to ask her name when she looks straight at me.

Adrenaline shoots through my veins. *Oh, sweet baby Jesus!*

"I know you," she says, her brows furrowing.

"You *know* her?" her petite friend asks, eyeing my Christmas sweater with contempt.

The woman's eyes slowly fill with recognition. "Yes. We went to junior high together, right?"

My throat tightens. I manage a weak nod.

She takes a step towards me. "What's your name?"

My cheeks flame. I know her name as if it were my own. "Kim Kincaid."

"Do you remember me, Kimberly?"

"Kim," I correct, unable to stop myself. "Rachel Davis. Yes, I remember you."

"Of course you would. But it's Rachel *Brooks* now, sweetie." Her smile thins as she touches her neck, flashing her diamond. "So how *are* you?"

"I'm fine," I say, desperately wishing Lisa had greeted them and not me. Here I am, facing my junior high nemesis with greasy hair scraped back into a ponytail, wearing the cheapest makeup and clothes on Earth. I probably look like a janitor.

"So I hear your sister is doing well," Rachel continues, her dark eyes glinting. "Isn't she a physician up in New York?"

"New Jersey," I say, wanting to die. How could she possibly know what Dena's doing? Is my sister popular even after high school?

"She must be so successful." Rachel smiles again. "Didn't I hear she married some history professor?"

"English," I say, trying not to sound defeated.

"NYU, wasn't it?"

"Columbia."

"Columbia!" her friend says. "Now *there's* a catch."

"So, Kim," Rachel says, arching her eyebrows. "Are *you* seeing anyone?"

"I am, actually," I reply, thankful to have something on their list of desirables.

"Really?" Rachel is clearly shocked. "And how long have you been seeing each other?"

"Two years."

"That's a long time," she says, then purposefully casts her eyes down to her diamond-studded finger. "It only took Will six weeks to propose. We were married in three months."

"Your wedding was *gorgeous*," her friend purrs.

Rachel gives a faint nod, her eyes never leaving mine. "So, have you two talked about marriage?"

Sweat trickles down my neck. I glance at Larry's door, willing him to stride out like he usually does and call, "Kim! I need you back here."

"Well?" Rachel prompts. "Don't you talk about it?"

"No," I say. "Not really."

The friend shakes her head. "Doesn't sound good."

"*Leanne*," Rachel chastises, although she certainly doesn't mean it. "Leave her alone. Can't you see we've invaded her privacy enough?"

"Please," I beg, near tears. Their smiles evaporate and they look at me curiously. "Just let me tell Mr. Mitchell that you're here."

I turn on my heel and take the seven steps to Paul's door, knocking lightly. "There's a Rachel Davis here for you," I say through the crack.

"Who?"

"Sorry. Brooks. Rachel *Brooks*."

"Oh, great," he calls. "Tell her to come in."

I watch the two women saunter inside and it's as if I'm back in junior high, unpopular and as dumpy as ever. While so much has changed in my life, even more has remained exactly the same.

Chapter Ten

"Dirty Mexican."

I jump and nearly drop the books that I've been pulling from my locker. Rachel Davis laughs as she and her worshiping throng passes by me, articulating other racial slurs all the way down the hall. I don't know why they call me this. I've told Rachel a dozen times that I'm Puerto Rican—and actually only *part*—but she never listens. They love to call me "Dirty Mexican" or "Buck Teeth." This last one is because my front teeth have a gap and I have an overbite. But Mom says that once she can afford it, she'll get me braces, so hopefully that name, at least, will die away.

With a sigh, I shove the books into my book bag and start for class. I think of Rachel and how pretty she is while the rest of us are struggling with acne and periods and growth spurts and breasts. She seems to have it all, and perfectly. Her hair is always shiny and flawlessly auburn, she's just the right height—five six—and she's thin and has great boobs and the boys fawn over her as if she's wearing a magic love potion.

At lunch I sit with my few friends, and we are all nerds. There are three levels of female popularity in our class of ninety students. The Queen Bee is Rachel Davis, her reign endless and cruel. We call Rachel and her slew of friends "The Royal Snob Brigade," and they gleefully earn their moniker. After them are "The Mixers". They'd love to be at the top but mostly linger in perpetual purgatory. Finally, there's us: the geeks, the nerds, the dorks of the grade—and I hold the absolute bottom rung. I'm here not because I'm super smart, but because I have no other choice. I don't have the looks, the money, or the connections to secure a spot in a better hierarchy.

So, I sit with the friends I'm lucky enough to have, eat my bologna and cheese sandwich, and try not to get noticed.

After lunch, I stop by the water fountain for a drink. I sense movement behind me, but before I can move, warm soda pours over my head. I turn and it is Rachel, proudly tossing away an empty Diet Coke can. She laughs, and her two blonde friends laugh, and she says, "Stupid Mexican bitch."

My skin flames. Mean words crowd into my mouth. But when she meets my eyes, helplessness seizes me. I shake like a dog cowering before its abusive owners and say nothing.

"Do you even speak English, spic?" she says, smirking at me. "*¿Hablamos español?*"

Everyone knows I'm not fluent in Spanish, that I only look like it. But from the little I know, Rachel said, "Do *we* speak Spanish?" and it gives me a certain thrill to know that she can't even form a proper sentence. But my little smile has a dark look cross her face.

"What? You got something to say, Buck Teeth?"

Her friends giggle. "Buck Teeth!"

My face flames and I shake my head, pick up my books, and walk away. This is all I ever do. I can never stand up to her. I know that. I have neither the courage, nor the words, to combat this witch, so I settle for turning and walking away. I used to think that

Rachel would tire of her game with me, but this has lasted for three years now and I doubt it'll ever end.

"See you later, *Kimberly*!" she taunts in the distance.

My face grows hotter. She knows I hate my full name, that everyone calls me Kim. I want to turn around and cuss her out, maybe pound her pretty face against the wall.

Oh, who am I kidding? I think as I turn on the faucet at the bathroom sink, hating myself as I scrub the sticky Diet Coke from my hair and shirt.

I'm just Kim Kincaid: ugly loser, dateless wonder, who looks like a Puerto Rican and can't even speak Spanish.

Chapter Eleven

MONDAY, DECEMBER 12, 2005

"I need the one with the cover letter overnighted," Larry says, handing me two manila envelopes and a signed, crisp letter. "Here's the address. It's important. Do you think we can make it?"

I glance at the clock: 5:12 p.m. The pickup's in three minutes and I'd promised to pick up Summer in eighteen. "I can try," I say, quickly logging onto the FedEx homepage. My fingers fly across the keyboard as I enter the addresses and I wait anxiously for the label to print. Larry watches everything from a chair near my desk as sweat pearls across my forehead.

"There!" I say, smoothing the label on the package and dumping the contents inside. I race out of the office and down the flights of stairs into the cold and darkening evening. I see the mail van in the distance and race to the deliveryman just as he's putting the van into gear. "Wait! One more!" I cry, scrambling to the passenger side and wishing luck had given me Jared instead of this stranger.

"You made it," says a husky, fortyish man. He gives me a wink. "In a hurry?"

"You can say that," I say, breathless, as I hand the envelope to him. "Thanks!" I turn and race back into the building. I did it! I accomplished something important for my boss! He'll congratulate me for sure, which is a rarity in this thankless job.

"Did you make it?" Larry asks as I stroll triumphantly into his office.

"Just barely," I say with a wide grin.

"Good job."

I return his cheesy thumbs-up sign and retreat to my desk, where I notice the second manila envelope sitting in my chair. *What if...?* But I don't finish the thought because I've suddenly gone cold all over.

I pick up the envelope and remove its contents. The topmost paper is a cover letter. *I mailed the wrong one!*

"Jesus!" The packages had been identical. It was an understandable mistake...

"What's wrong?" Larry calls from his office.

I anxiously show him the offending letter. "I accidentally switched the packages."

His face darkens. "How will the attorney know what to do without a letter, Kim?"

I try to recover. "Should I try to catch the FedEx guy before he leaves?"

"Do what you have to." He turns his chair around so his back faces me.

The FedEx truck is just pulling away when I sprint outside. "Wait!" I'm waving my arms like a lunatic. "Wait!"

The van slows, then pulls to a stop next to the sidewalk. I race over, my face hot and clammy. "Back already?" the driver says with another wink.

"I'm so sorry," I say, then shakily bring up the manila envelope. "I mailed the wrong package. Is there any way I can switch this out?"

"I don't know," he says, looking doubtful. "That's not really our protocol..."

My heart sinks. "*Please*. My boss is going to kill me." The image of Larry's face fills my mind. Even though I hate my job, the threat of being fired is a thousand times worse.

The man looks back in his van. "Okay," he relents. "I *did* see you mail it." He stands and fishes through the box of packages. When he returns with my envelope, I rip off the address label and affix it to the correct one.

"Thank you, thank you!" I exclaim, disbelieving that I'd made it in time, that something has actually worked out for me.

"It's no problem." He's eyeing me now. "You know, after all this, I think a nice dinner is just the ticket for you."

"Dinner?" I look at him in confusion.

"With me. I'd like to take you to dinner."

"Oh. No, I'm sorry," I say, flustered. "I already have a boyfriend."

He shakes his head. "Figures."

"Thanks, though," I say, grateful for the compliment. It's been a long time since anybody's asked me out. I wave at him and start back for my building.

Way to go, me! I think, jubilant with relief. *I did something right!*

When I return, Larry is picking up his leather attaché case and doesn't even notice me come in. "I did it!" I announce with a grand smile.

He looks up. "Oh. Well, now that I think about it, that letter could have waited until morning to go out. Still, it's good that you fixed your mistake." He drops a stack of draft affidavits into my arms and strolls for the door. "If you can make the revisions I've marked, that'd be great." He grabs his trench coat and slips it over his shoulders.

"You're heading out?" I cast a surreptitious glance at the clock.

It's 5:16 P.M. His calendar had noted him leaving early, but I figured since everyone else had gone home that Larry would let me off early as well.

No such luck. He fastens the buttons of his coat and picks up his briefcase. "Yeah. Sorry to bail on you, but I wanted to see my wife and kids before it gets dark."

"Oh. Right." I gaze down at my cluttered desk, then back at the clock. Single people get no sympathy. What can I possibly want to get home to, anyway? I've no husband, no children. No life, apparently.

Larry heads out the door with a curt wave, and I immediately drop the affidavits on top of my desk. Maybe I can't leave early, but I'll be damned if I'm going to work on anything more tonight. If Larry can leave, then obviously this crap isn't that important.

I look around my desk for something to do. Bored with Solitaire and having exhausted all possible knowledge of celebrity gossip, I'm ready for anything to swallow the time. I notice Lisa has a trashy romance novel doubling as a paperweight and I bring it to my desk. Even though it's always been one of my New Year's resolutions, I've never really liked to read (that's Dena's M.O.). With a sigh, I crack open the pages and trudge through a few paragraphs, perpetually glancing at the clock until it's my time to go. Then I mechanically slip on my coat, turn off the lights, and lock the door.

The administration building is completely empty, even though all the hall lights are on. I'm usually the last one out of the building unless my bosses decide to pull all-nighters and it is rather lonely. The air always feels eerily electric at this time of night. That's probably because I know that if I'm murdered, no one will know until morning.

I slip into the stairwell and make my way to the bottom floor when a voice from below makes me jump.

"America, America, God bless these pants on me!" bellows a

deep, Japanese-accented voice. I peer around the corner and see an unfamiliar cleaning man tapping his feet to the beat of "America the Beautiful" as he swirls a mop against the tiled floor.

"Oh!" he cries when he spots me. His cheeks flush with embarrassment. "So sorry. Didn't see you."

"It's okay." I take a few steps toward the door.

"You on way home?"

"Yes."

He smiles kindly. "Have a nice night with the family, Miss."

I return his smile, wishing I had a family to go home to. But then I realize that I have Summer, and she *is* my family, so I guess that's a start.

At 5:42 p.m.—later than I'd promised, but I figure Summer's too young to understand the concept of time, much less late pickups—I'm back at Ben & Jerri's heading towards the room where the receptionist told me the children were building Play-Doh castles.

I pause at a small Dutch door and peer inside, my gaze shifting among the children until my eyes lock onto Summer's spiraled hair, a slight frown touching her face as she focuses on rolling a pink ball between her hands.

Bethany sees me and strolls over. "You're earlier than most," she says, leaning her hip against the doorframe.

"Really?" *Seems awfully late to me.* "How was Summer?"

Bethany follows my gaze. "At first it was hard. But then she calmed down and started playing with the other kids. She's very creative with art."

"Really? That's cool." Perhaps my niece will be a famous sculptress. Or the next Van Gogh.

Bethany grins. "We've given a project to all the kids to finish by the end of the week. She seems really into it."

Just then, Summer glances up and sees me. "Aunt Kim!" she cries, struggling to stand, then cautiously places her mold of Play-Doh on a shelf before rushing over. Bethany opens the wooden door for her. "Are we going home?"

"Yup," I say, as she wraps herself around my knees. *This is life,* I think. *This is what I've been missing.* I pick her up and Summer squeezes me tight. "Let's go home."

I toss my keys onto the breakfast table as Summer trots toward the television.

"Can I watch *Cinderella*?" she asks without turning around.

"Sure," I say, wondering what fascination the film holds for her. I press PLAY on the remote. The screen flickers and after a few seconds, the TV fills with pastel colors to the accompaniment of a string orchestra.

As I walk into the kitchen, I notice the answering machine is blinking. I half-listen to a series of telemarketers and finally the mechanical "End of messages."

Jared still hasn't called. It's been two days since he'd stormed out of my apartment and not one word since.

I wonder if I should try calling him again to apologize. Now that I think about it, I had reacted just like all those psycho girlfriends I absolutely abhor. I wonder what he's doing. Does he miss me? Is he staring at the phone like I am right now?

I know what I have to do. I press the speed dial on my phone and wait in the silence.

"Hello?"

"He's still not called."

"Ugh," Jillian moans. "What an asshole."

In a moment of weakness, I'd e-mailed Jillian during my lunch break and spilled the news on Jared. She's usually a receptive audience, but with Jared, she can be a little unforgiving. "He's not an—" I lower my voice to a whisper, "—*asshole*. I treated him pretty badly, you know."

"Oh Kim, come *on*! You had better get a reality check."

"So, how's the affair with your boss going?" I return sardonically.

"Ha ha. Totally different. He's not my boyfriend."

"Oh? Since when?"

"Since always."

"So what do you call him then?"

There's a pause as she considers this. "I guess my lover."

I blow out an exasperated sigh. "I think somebody else needs a reality check."

"And anyway," she continues, unabated, "I'm not the one under the microscope right now. You are."

"What are you talking about?"

"I think you'd better wake up to who your man is, Kim. And fast."

My heart instantly tightens. I have a fear that I cannot express, not even to Jillian. "And you know who he is?"

"Yes. Not good for you."

I blow out the breath I'd been holding. "Okay then. I'm hanging up..."

"Please, Kim. You have got to see that all he ever does is disappoint you. You're unhappy!"

"I'm not unhappy."

"You are! Are you even listening to yourself?"

"Will you get off my back already?" I hiss in low tones, throwing a glance over at Summer. Thankfully, she's still engrossed in her movie, as if Disney is some sort of catnip for children. "I called for some sympathy, not a freaking lecture."

She sighs. "Okay, okay. I'm sorry. I just want what's best for you."

"And I want you to be my friend for a few minutes and empathize."

"Okay." She takes a breath. "So the bastard hasn't called. What are you going to do?"

I slip into a chair and draw my knees into my chest. "I dunno. Wait for him to call?"

"That's such a passive attitude. Why don't you call him?"

"I already tried. No, I can't call him again. I'd look pathetic."

"What do you want to do, then?"

"I'm—I'm going to find him."

"Find him? As in, right now?"

"Sure," I say, both excited and anxious about my sudden decision. "It'd be the grand gesture. Really show him I care, and that I'm sorry. Maybe I'll even cook him dinner. You know how long it's been since I've done that?"

"I don't know, Kim..."

"Nope. You can't change my mind."

"Okay. Just be careful."

"Why do I need to be careful?"

"I don't want you getting more hurt."

"I won't," I assure her, although I'm getting annoyed. "Listen, I better go before I lose all courage to do this. Wish me luck?"

"Good luck," she says half-heartedly. "Let me know if you need help with the kid."

"But you hate babysitting."

She gives a dry chuckle. "Honey, for you, I'd try my best not to hate it. That's love, right there."

"Okay." I'm smiling despite myself. "Later."

"Bye."

I click off the phone and revert my attention to my niece. "Summer?"

"Uh huh?"

"Come on." I retrieve my purse. "We're going out."

She stands up, suddenly looking jubilant. "Can I wear my tutu?"

"Sorry," I say as I snatch up the keys. "Not tonight."

Chapter Twelve

Summer's strapped to her booster seat, swinging her legs so hard her motions rattle the entire backseat. "Excited?" I call, glancing at her in the rearview mirror.

"Yeah!" she exclaims. "I love car rides!"

I scan the radio stations, finally settling on classic rock. U2's "Beautiful Day" beats through the cabin and I try to sing along, but my voice fades quickly. I can't shake the feeling that something's wrong and that I'm throwing myself headfirst into a hurricane.

We arrive at Jared's apartment complex and I park between a vacant handicapped spot and a blue Mazda. I lean over the armrest to unbuckle Summer and as I do so, a light from a nearby lamppost falls over my shaking hands. Summer pulls open the door and leaps from the car. I walk around and she grasps for my hand, and together we make our way up the two flights of stairs to Jared's front door. The pinecone and flower wreath I'd bought him hangs slanted just above the peephole. There's two logs of newspapers on the WELCOME, FRIEND! doormat (also bought by me). My palms are slick with sweat, so I drop Summer's hand to clasp one of her tiny shoulders.

She glances up at me and our gazes hold for a few moments before she lets out a protracted sigh. "So, what are we waiting for?"

I square my shoulders. If Jared's home, I'll apologize and swear to make it up to him by any means necessary. If he isn't, I'll simply write a long, heart-felt apology and leave it on the counter for him to find. Then I'll keep calling him until he forgives me and we're back to normal again.

I'm about to push my key into the lock when I hear a muffled thump past the door. Then something else. Laughter? A sudden chill races across my skin, but it's not because of the frosty wind.

"Aunt Kim?"

"Wait," I tell her as I fish for my cell. I press for his number and wait in the silence.

The trill of his phone tinkles past the door from the living room. It rings on and on until it stops and I'm put to voicemail.

"Hey, this is Jared," comes his scratchy voice. "I'm not in, so leave—"

I snap the phone closed.

Another thump. The unmistakable sound of muffled voices.

"Come on," I say to Summer, turning us around and hastily making our way down the flight of stairs. My legs are moving on their own accord. I just need to get out of there as quickly as possible.

"Where are we going?" Summer asks.

"Back home," I say, knowing the pressure behind my eyes has only seconds before its release. We reach the car and I hastily unlock the doors and haul her back inside.

"Aunt Kim?" She looks worried now.

"I'm fine, I'm fine." I try to sound reassuring, but I'm smiling through a storm of salty tears. "It's fine. Here we go." I buckle her in and shut the door, then walk around to the driver's side. I glance up at Jared's door, just visible over the railing, before I pull myself inside.

I don't know what just happened. *Those noises...* I shake my head. *No. They could have been anything.*

But why didn't he answer his phone?

"We're fine," I tell Summer as I wipe my eyes and turn on the ignition. We start up the street and I say with forced cheerfulness, "So. What do you feel like for dinner?"

"Calzones?" Summer replies uncertainly.

"Calzones it is then." I am in such a mood that she could have said "crème brûlée" and I'd have conjured it up just to make one of us happy. I check my reflection in the visor and fix my wayward hair, then turn on the radio. Anything to keep my mind from really thinking about what just happened.

We cut across a long stretch of empty road and a few snowflakes drift across the windshield. I flick on the wipers and turn up the heat.

"Snow!" Summer cries, breaking the silence. "Can we play in the snow?"

My smile is small, but at least it is there. "It may take a while for us to play in it, seeing as it's not much right now. But sure. What do you want to do?"

"Make snow angels. And have a snowball fight!"

"Sounds great," I say, and it does. "And then afterward I can make us some hot chocolate. How does that sound?"

Summer claps her hands excitedly. Then suddenly she exclaims, "Look, Aunt Kim! Christmas trees!"

There's a parking lot a few blocks away choked with families pawing through dozens of Douglas firs. I haven't had a real Christmas tree since my mother died. These last few years, I experienced tree ownership vicariously through Jillian, who has this gorgeous fake tree with white pine needles. Jared, of course, has no tree, which is fine since he stacks his presents anywhere—mostly in bed.

"Do you have a Christmas tree?" Summer asks.

I glance at her eager reflection in the mirror. "Nope." Inspiration hits me. "Do you want to go look?"

"Yes, yes, yes!"

I laugh as we swing into the drive. After we park, I pull her out and we join the ranks of elated children and weary parents making their final selections. Summer bounds in front of me for the largest of the firs, before I explain to her that my apartment cannot accommodate so large a tree (nor can my wallet).

We walk down the slender aisles together. Summer flits from tree to tree while I breathe in the evergreens' relaxing perfume. I reach out and touch some long, waxy needles, noticing that my hands are reddening from the cold. I reach into my purse for my gloves and graze my box of Virginia Slims, which through sheer force of will I've avoided touching since Summer's arrival. Well, there was that cigarette at 3 a.m.—the one I'd taken about four puffs from alone and outside my apartment—but that hardly counts.

I'm the laziest smoker I know. I don't even need one every day, but still can't fully kick the habit. Seeing them now makes my mouth ache, so I quickly light one between my teeth and inhale deeply. *I'm going to have to quit these for good,* I decide for probably the millionth time, although something about tonight makes it seem possible. I'm just stamping out the cigarette when Summer lets out a whoop of triumph.

"This one!" she exclaims, grasping the bough of a fir as if it's a hand.

It's perfect: less than six feet tall, not very wide, and finely proportioned. It reminds me of the trees my mother used to purchase for Dena and me when we were kids, and the memory warms my insides.

I stop the man in a checkered sweater. "Excuse me? Sir? We'd like to take this one."

He smiles and switches his gaze between us. "Sure, Miss. That's a lovely choice. How about you bring your car around? After we settle the bill, I'll strap it to the roof for you."

"Sure," I say, wondering how much it is as I take up Summer's hand and race back to the car. The man graciously pulls the tree onto the roof himself, even giving us two tethers for the ride home. I pay the astronomical seventy dollar price from the two hundred Dena allotted for Summer's food, rationalizing that Summer seems to like my food just fine.

We drive home listening to the radio and singing along to "Rudolph the Red-Nosed Reindeer." Summer is clapping her hands and swinging her feet and I realize that I'm happy. I haven't felt so good in a long, long time.

I almost forget about Jared. *Almost*.

It's as we pull into the parking lot that I wonder how the hell we're getting the tree into my apartment. I've never had the foresight of Dena, who is lucky enough to have a dependable man strong enough to drag a tree up a flight of stairs.

Summer and I get out of the car and survey the tree for a few minutes. I look at the long, narrow stairwell to my door. The tree suddenly looks as large and unwieldy as a refrigerator.

"What are we going to do?" Summer asks with grave concern.

The guy who sold us this monster probably thought I had a man to help me. Of course, I was also stupid not to think of this beforehand. But it's easier to blame the world for insisting everyone buy enormous Christmas trees, or require that they live in homes with main floor access, or at least a footman.

I stand with my hands tucked into my jacket pockets, my bottom lip caught between my teeth, thinking.

An affable voice calls from behind us. "Do you need some help?"

Summer and I jump and turn simultaneously. Behind us is a thirtyish man with short brown hair wearing round, silver-rimmed glasses that catch in the overhead light. I've seen him around a few times before, but don't know his name. From a distance he seemed nondescript, but closer up I realize he's kind of cute.

His smile is warm and friendly as he strides over to us. "I can help, if you want. You seem to be stuck."

I look up at the tree, then back at him. "Are you sure?"

As his smile broadens, two dimples appear on either side of his mouth. "It's really no trouble."

"Okay." I watch as he effortlessly untethers the tree and directs me to balance the trunk as he guides it off my car.

"There!" His breath comes out in white puffs as his gloved hands dive into the conifer. "Which way?"

"Up here," I say, taking Summer's hand as we ascend the stairs first.

"I'm Brandon," he says between breaths.

"I'm Kim," I call over my shoulder. Has my voice always sounded that high-pitched? "This is my niece, Summer."

"You ready for Christmas, Summer?"

"Oh, yes!" she exclaims. "I can't wait for the presents."

He laughs as we finish the last few stairs and start down the narrow walkway. "I really can't thank you enough," I say as I search for my keys. "I had no idea how to get it up here."

"It's no problem." His eyes are like patches of sky, and very kind.

"So," I say, trying to think of polite conversation, "do you live here?"

"Nope." He rights the tree and waits for me to open the door. When I do, he slides it inside and says, "I'm just visiting my sister. Where do you want this?"

"Um..." I survey the cramped apartment and quickly settle on a nook between the breakfast table and hallway, just in front of the small coat closet. "Over there is fine."

He picks it up and brings it over, then looks around curiously. "Where's your tree stand?"

Shit. "Oh. I don't have one." I giggle to cover my embarrassment. "Probably should have thought of that first, right?"

Brandon chuckles and adjusts his glasses. "It's okay. Just go buy a cheap one and bring it back. I can help if you just—"

"No, it's okay," I say, slightly disarmed by his presence. Because —between my nervous laughter and sweaty palms—I suddenly realize that I'm attracted to him. "I can take care of it from here."

"You sure? It's really no problem—"

"Thanks again for your help." I smile as I show him to the door. I know my feelings are wrong—I love Jared—and decide the best solution is to get him out fast.

"Okay." He smiles down at me. "So, will I see you around, Kim?"

"Maybe." I clear my throat. "Anyway, thanks again. And have a great Christmas."

"You too." He turns to Summer. "Merry Christmas, kiddo."

"Merry Christmas!" she calls, watching us.

Brandon smiles one last time before ducking out. I shut and lock the door behind him.

"I like him," Summer says with a wide grin. "He's nice."

"I guess so." I try to sound casual as I return my attention to the tree. "Okay, babe. Looks like we need a few things. Feel up to some quick shopping?"

"Another car ride?"

"If you can bear it."

"Then wait!" She rushes from the room and returns with her tutu. "Can I wear this now? *Please?*"

"What the heck." I bend to help her put it on. "'Tis the Christmas season."

Chapter Thirteen

TUESDAY, DECEMBER 13TH, 2005

"I think it's looking good," I say the following evening as Summer and I stand back to admire our work. After a tremendous struggle, I secured the fir into a new red metal base. I also purchased a half-priced crimson and green skirt that forms a perfect fan around the lowermost boughs. We've strung six lines of multi-colored lights that blink cheerily against the green pine needles. And—in a moment of inspiration—I'd brewed a batch of hot chocolate and rustled up an old copy of Kenny G's holiday album, which fills the apartment with a jubilant saxophone that Summer and I decorate to. My apartment now has the warm, festive ambiance of a proper home.

"Let's get the ornaments!" Summer exclaims.

"Right." I walk over to the shopping bags and pull out an assortment of bulbs. How could I resist? I'd initially limited myself to less than thirty dollars for the lot, but when the price nearly exceeded the tree, I rationalize a real Christmas was overdue. And as Summer and I hang the ornaments off the tips of branches, I've already forgotten the cost and am solely enjoying the experience.

There comes an unexpected knock on the front door. Summer, clutching an armful of bulbs, looks at me questioningly.

"Wait here," I instruct, setting my ornaments on the kitchen table and walking to the door. I peer through the peephole and see a Razorback hat. "Jared?"

"Hey!" he calls. "I wanted to make sure you were home first."

I hear the key scratching in the lock and take one step back before Jared has me in his arms, kissing me passionately. "Oh!" I gasp, my stomach lurching with surprise, relief, and annoyance. "I —"

"These are for you." He proudly hands me a dozen red carnations tied with a white bow.

My heart vibrates with happiness, but still there is a nagging suspicion tugging at the back of my mind. I have so many questions, but no idea how to voice them. "Thank you," I say, holding the flowers in a feeble grasp.

"And don't think I forgot about you, tyke," he says to Summer. From his jacket, he produces a white polar bear, the likes of which appear on Coca Cola Christmas ads.

"Oh, that's sweet," I say, motioning for Summer to come forward, which she reluctantly does after setting down her stash of ornaments. "What do you say, Summer?"

"Thank you." Her voice is low and guarded.

Jared doesn't appear to notice her reservation as he presses the bear into her small arms, "So I wanted to say that I got your messages and realized how much I missed you." He lets this sink in. Then he pushes himself against me and kisses me again. This time I taste the beer and smoke on his breath, and nausea squirms in my stomach. Keenly aware that Summer's watching everything, I push him away—something I've never done before.

Jared seems a little put off by this, but quickly recovers. "Anyway, I thought we could get some pizza and maybe catch a movie."

"Right now?"

"Sure. Why not?"

I gesture towards Summer. "Do you have something in mind that's appropriate for her?"

He sighs wearily. "Can't you get a babysitter or something? Come on, Kim. I haven't seen you in forever."

That was your choice, I think, remembering my walk with Alice in the park, her description of her husband fending off responsibility like a swarm of gnats. "*I'm* her babysitter, Jared. Don't you get it?"

"Fine, fine. We'll just get pizza." He winks mischievously. "And then I thought we could go to bed early, if you know what I mean."

He stares deep into my eyes as his thumbs trace circles on my arms. My skin prickles with sudden heat. Jared always has that effect on me, no matter what mood I'm in. One glance is all it takes. "Okay," I hear myself saying. "Pizza sounds great."

Jared is nearly asleep when I return from checking on Summer, who is snug beneath the covers on the foldout couch, breathing softly. "She's asleep," I whisper as I shut the bedroom door.

Jared blinks awake and pushes himself up. I admire his broad, naked chest. Sometimes it's hard to believe he's my boyfriend. He smiles and pats the space beside him. "Come here."

As I crawl into bed, I pull at my red silk negligee—something I only wear when Jared stays over—uncertain why I'm so anxious. I breathe in his scent: a mingling of Coors Light, vanilla cigars, and shaving cream. All of which I usually find intoxicating, but now leaves me a little queasy.

I want to confront him about where he's been and why he

hasn't called me, but the questions die on my tongue as he pulls me in for a kiss.

"I've missed you," he mumbles against my throat.

"Me too," I say, meaning it. I don't think he knows how much I've missed him, how much I've worried.

We make love in under ten minutes, in all of our usual positions, but I'm so disconnected I don't even orgasm. It didn't help that I kept shushing Jared anytime he made a noise in fear that we mights scar Summer for life.

Jared falls back against the pillows and exhales. "That was nice," he says, and then reaches over my bare breasts for his lighter and pack of Marlboros sitting on the nightstand.

He offers me a cigarette, but I shake my head. "No thanks. I'm trying to quit."

"Yeah. Good luck with that." He lights it quickly and exhales.

"Can you blow that outside? I just had the place cleaned."

He gives me a pointed look, but stands from the bed and obligingly opens the window a few inches. He exhales through the screen, takes two more puffs, and quickly stamps out the cigarette in the ready ashtray.

As he settles back for sleep, I lean over and say, "Jared?"

"Hmmm?"

"Did you notice I didn't come?"

"What?" He rolls over to face me. His eyes are tired and red.

I normally wouldn't say anything, but I want to feel *something*. I hate it when he orgasms and I don't. It's almost like I'm a machine that he uses for one purpose. "I didn't come. I was wondering if maybe you could..." My eyes lower to my thighs, hoping that he might get the idea.

"Are you for real?" he asks, flummoxed.

"Yes. It's been months since you've gone down on me, and I do it to you all the time." All true, and incredibly frustrating. I pause before I add self-righteously, "I think it's time for my turn, don't you?"

"Fine, whatever." He yawns, stretches, and then slowly crawls between my legs.

I lean back on the pillows and try to focus on the pleasant sensations, but after a minute, they fade. Moments later, they're nonexistent. "Jared?" I say, sitting up.

He's fast asleep between my legs, forehead pressed against my chubby inner thigh.

Oh my god. No man has ever fallen asleep on me like this. What will Jillian say when she finds out? This is beyond embarrassing. This is—actually, I cannot fully articulate the degree of my mortification. All I know is that whatever I'm feeling is rapidly morphing into anger and resentment. "Wake up, Jared," I say, moving my leg a little so that his face bobs onto the fitted bed sheet.

He blinks awake and immediately wriggles to his designated spot on the bed, throwing his arm over my chest as he spoons up behind me.

"You fell asleep," I say, waiting in the silence for him to answer. I wait thirty seconds. Then I shake his shoulder. "Jared. Wake up."

He opens one lazy eye, then promptly closes it. "Come on, Kim. Go to sleep. Shit, you're so fucking demanding." He turns to the wall and is snoring within seconds.

My face reddens with shame. In quick, jerky movements, I pull on my nightgown, sweatpants, and long-sleeved shirt, dive my feet into a pair of slippers, grab my pillow and stomp from the room.

As I shut the door, I realize this will be the first night that Jared and I sleep separately in the same apartment. The first time in the two years we've been together. I'm suddenly having doubts, and nearly go back when the anger returns with a vengeance. *How could he have fallen asleep like that? Is he drunk? How much has he been drinking? And with whom?*

But I breathe out these questions and decide to leave it for the morning. I clutch my pillow to my chest and creep out into the dark living room, where Summer's silhouette is faint in the moonlight.

I crawl in next to her warm body and she turns around in her sleep and snuggles right against me. In all the times Jared has embraced me, I've never felt more comfortable and at peace than I do now.

And even though worry and fear are clawing at my heart, at least for now, I am safe.

And loved.

The next morning, I hear my alarm go off for work in the distance. I slip off the couch—making sure not to wake Summer—and return to my bedroom, where Jared is sound asleep in a tangle of pillows and bed sheets. I turn off the alarm, mechanically swallow my Pill, and stare down at him hard.

I love him. I know I do. But does he love me? And if he does, why doesn't he ever say it?

And where has he been all this time?

Is he cheating on me?

The last question sends a chill through my veins. I gaze down at Jared, thinking about all these questions, wondering if I'll ever know the answers.

Jared sighs and stretches, then opens his eyes to look up at me. "What are you doing?" he asks, sitting up.

I cross my arms. "Nothing."

"Come here." He grins as he pulls open the comforter. He winks mischievously and I notice he has his usual morning hard on.

"You want to have *sex?*" My eyes widen in disbelief. Doesn't he know something's wrong? Is he that dense, or does he just not care?

"Sure!" He brings up his hand to tug at my arm. "Come here. We can have a quickie before you go to work, like we used to."

Unbelievable! I take a step back, away from his touch. He hasn't even noticed that we slept apart. All he cares about is having sex.

His grin disappears. "What's wrong with you?"

"Nothing." I make the three steps to my bureau, which I furiously rip open. "I've got to get Summer to daycare and get to work. You can let yourself out, right?"

"I guess," he says, his eyes following me as I dress. "Are you okay?"

"I'm fine," I say, wishing at the same time that he'd press the matter and discover what's really wrong. But he doesn't. He never does.

"Okay. Well, Maggie is having another party tonight. You feel like going?"

Exasperation quickens my tongue. "Didn't you just go to a party? What is it with you and these parties?"

"What's the big deal?" he demands, all happiness gone. "You used to love going out. Getting drunk was your middle name."

"Not anymore." I sigh, turning from him.

"What is *with* you?" He sounds genuinely confused. "I thought you loved all this."

"I used to..."

"Then what's changed?"

Me! I want to scream. *I've changed!* "Nothing," I say instead. "Sorry."

"So, do you want to go or not?"

"I can't. I have to take care of Summer." Glaring at each other, I realize just how my priorities have shifted in such a short amount of time.

"Okay. Fine." I can tell that he's already sulking. He swings his long legs out of bed and starts pulling on his clothes. "Then I'll go for both of us. You call me whenever you decide that I'm worth your time. Maybe once your niece is gone, you'll be interested in getting our life back to the way it used to be."

"Fine," I say, but I'm not sure if I want my old life. I'm so angry and disappointed that I have to turn away before he sees the burning tears. *He doesn't know me. He really doesn't know me at all.*

Then I wonder if I actually know *him*. If I've somehow fabricated our love together. Built a life with delusions and one-sided hope—all expiring.

My Jared, the love of my life, the man I want to marry, suddenly seems nothing more substantial than a puff of smoke. A shadow on the wall. A complete and total stranger.

And I have no idea what to do.

Chapter Fourteen

THURSDAY, MAY 6, 1993

"Hey, sexy," Ben Harris slurs, pushing me up against the locker with his massive arms. He stinks of rancid sweat, stale deodorant, and crushed grass. His grin is ferocious—like he'll eat me up. Enjoy chewing me bit by bit.

I'm trapped, but try not to show my fear. Classes already started, so we're alone in the hallway.

"Please leave me alone," I whisper, half-heartedly pushing him away. But his body is like steel.

Ben's the football team's star quarterback and the most popular boy at school. He's also three years older than me and looms seven inches taller. I don't even know why he bothers with me, considering I'm so unpopular.

"How about we go to my place this weekend?" He rubs my waist with his hands, pinches my hips.

My breath comes in short, painful gasps. He's played this game with me for three months now. It had started so casually: him joining the chorus of Rachel and her friends with "Spic" or "Dirty Mexican." Then he started speaking to me privately, cruelly, when I was alone by my locker. The popular girls taunted me when they found out, fed by Rachel's rumor that I'm a slut who'll screw anybody given the chance, which is ironic because I am still a virgin who hasn't even French kissed a boy.

"I have a waterbed," Ben says, his breath moist and sticky on my neck. Then he tells me the many ways we will do it, and terror grips my heart. *Why's he doing this? And why can't I stop it?*

My arms hang useless as seaweed beside me. I close my eyes and think of Mom—who I haven't told because it'll hurt her too much —and pray to whoever's up there for help. Ben is going to rape me. I know it. Some day soon, when I am alone, he will force me to the ground or against a wall and I will lose my virginity to the most popular boy in high school in the most terrible way.

"Hey! You two should be in class!" calls a hall monitor.

Ben immediately steps back, then blows me a kiss. "Think about it," he says before he walks off.

I stare at the lockers until they become a gray, watery blur. I can't stand up to Rachel. I can't stand up to Ben. I just accept whatever fate doles out, because I don't have the guts to do anything else.

Between classes, I stop at my locker and spin through its combination. The door clinks open and I return my English binder and paperbacks, then remove the enormous, white history textbook, which takes two hands to hold.

"Given any thought to this weekend?" comes a familiar voice and I stiffen.

I turn and Ben crushes me up against the locker. We aren't alone. There are five other boys circling us, most of whom I recognize from the football team. While one or two are quiet and look about anxiously, the rest are laughing and sneering at me, as if I'm a wounded animal on the side of the road they'd like to hit with a rock or pull apart for the fun of it.

Ben pushes against my thighs, gropes between my legs. "How 'bout it, baby? Just you and me on the 'ol water bed, doing it like animals? Huh? You'd like that, wouldn't you?" His breath is hot on my neck. "*Wouldn't you?*"

Something clicks inside, like the correct combination to a lock. My fingers inch around for the history book, gripping it so tightly my knuckles ache. With a scream that leaves my throat raw, I bring it around and smash the cover into Ben's unsuspecting face.

The boys around us stagger back in shock. When the book drops away, Ben's face is bloody. He starts to cry.

I take off running. When I get to class, I slump at my desk and burst into tears, not caring that the teacher and other students are staring at me, or that my book's covered in Ben's snot and blood.

In minutes, there's a knock at the door, and the vice-principal steps inside. "Ms. Kincaid. Please come with me to my office."

Dena comes to pick me up at school about an hour later. The principal called my mother and said that I broke a student's nose and would have to be expelled, but once I told her and the principal what happened, my mother was furious and threatened to sue the school for its last penny. The principal found himself torn between my case and Ben's parental donations. Finally, he settled with having Ben suspended for three days, with the ability to make up home-work and tests. As a non-donating Puerto Rican family, it is the best we can do.

I see Dena in her used Honda Civic pull up to the curb and I pick up my book bag and stagger over. She's a junior at Rice University, home from finals. She is my mother's greatest pride, her boast to friends and co-workers. "My genius daughter," Mom will say with that special gleam in her eyes, "the future *doctor*!"

I've accepted that I'll never measure up to Dena. I have to carve out my place in the world, even though I am the most boring individual ever to step foot on it.

Dena leans over and pulls open the passenger door (we don't have automatic locks, much to Dena's embarrassment, since most of her peers drive BMWs and Audis). "Get in," she says.

I throw my book bag into the back seat, slide in, and close the door. We drive for a while in silence. Finally, Dena says, "Why didn't you tell us?"

My throat tightens. I never wanted Dena to know. Even with our poor background and Spanish looks, Dena is still beautiful. She was popular in high school and even popular at her ritzy college. She carries luck with her like a second shadow.

"I just didn't want you to know," I say at last, slipping out of my shoes and propping my bare feet on the glove compartment.

"Put your feet down," she says.

I obediently drop them.

"You still should have told us. It's not right what you've gone through."

"I just..." my voice trails.

She glances at me. "What?"

"I just wanted you to think I was popular."

Dena sighs as she eases the car onto the highway and switches lanes. "Popularity's not all it's cracked up to be, kiddo."

"I think it is."

Her laughter is devoid of mirth. "Well, how would you know?"

I open my mouth, but can think of nothing to say.

She picks up her hand, hesitates, and then rests it awkwardly on my thigh. "I'm sorry," she says softly. "If I'd been there, I would've beaten that *maricon* to a pulp."

Dena rarely speaks Spanish. Hearing this word—albeit a horrible, derogatory one—makes me smile. I want so much to hold her hand, like we did when we were kids. I want to tell her everything about Ben and Rachel. How every day at school cuts me like ground glass. How I just want to disappear.

I slide my left hand over so that my fingertips are just brushing hers. "Thanks," I say.

She smiles and I think she's going to say something else, something that will lift my spirits, some nugget of wisdom that will get me through my final years of high school. But she says, "So. I met the most wonderful guy the other day."

"Oh?" I say, and listen with feigned interest as she tells me about a boy that liked her on sight and how she thinks she will go out with him. I retract my hand, which doesn't faze her, and turn to stare out the window. My time is done. Once again, the world reverts to Dena. And in a few minutes, it'll be like I'm not even there.

Chapter Fifteen

WEDNESDAY, DECEMBER 14, 2005

"I don't even know if I still love him," I say to Jillian in despair, but don't cry when I say this because I've run out of tears. We are sitting on her Chesterfield leather couch in her condominium's living room. Cool sunshine falls in dusty pillars onto the pseudooriental carpeting and frost eats at the corners of her bay windows. I'd called Jillian for an emergency get-together and she—being the best friend that she is—picked me up just outside my office building during lunch and rushed me to her home.

"What happened?" She folds her legs into her chest, her eyes wide and sad. "You always said you were certain that you loved him."

"And now I'm having doubts." I lean against the cool leather of the couch and pull the red cashmere afghan around my shoulders. "We're just so different. I never saw it before. I think I turned myself into who he wanted, not into who I wanted to be. Do you know what I mean?"

"I have some idea," Jillian says, then stands to retrieve our steaming mugs of hot chocolate from the microwave. She splashes in some Baileys Irish Cream and hands one to me. "Here, sweetie. Drink up. It'll make you feel better."

I gaze down at my mug and let out a light laugh. "You even put in my favorite jumbo marshmallows."

"Nothing's too good for my favorite guest," she says, repositioning herself on the couch and taking a long, contemplative sip. "Seriously, though. I wish you weren't feeling so bad."

I follow her example, taking a few cautious sips. The hot chocolate warms me to my toes and my mood lifts. I wrap my arms around my legs and balance the mug on my knees. "I dunno. The sex last night was so awkward, so...nothing. There was hardly any love in it at all."

"You felt like a machine again, didn't you?" The sadness in her eyes deepens.

"Yeah." I look away. "And when he fell asleep during—"

"*Totally* unforgivable," she cuts in, unable to stop herself.

I sigh. "Jillian, what should I do? Should I break up with him?"

"I can't tell you what to do, honey." She reaches out to stroke my arm.

"But if you were in my place," I insist. "Would you stay? Or would you leave?"

She shrugs. "I don't know. And anyway, I don't think I'm in the position to dole out any sort of relationship advice. Especially considering that I'm still very much involved with my married boss."

"How's that going?" I ask, somewhat relieved to be out of the spotlight.

"Well, I think I'm understanding my position better." She stops and her face tightens. "I feel bad about this, you know? More so now than before. Like when his wife calls when we're at his house. I have to shut the hell up and not move an inch. And then I wonder what that poor woman—even if she is a bitch—would do if she found out. I'd..." Her voice trails and she sighs. "I don't know."

"So, are you still going to see him?"

"For now. Adam occasionally mentions leaving his wife. But I don't really know if I want that. Or him." She gives a faint shrug. "I guess we're in a similar boat."

"Seems so." A small smile touches my lips. I raise the steaming mug and take another sip.

"So this party Maggie is having tonight," Jillian says, reverting the spotlight back, "are you going or not?"

I shake my head. "I already told him I wasn't."

"So? Why don't you check it out? That way, you can see what he's like when you're not there."

I can't help but laugh. "You want me to spy on him?"

"Sure!" She says this as if it's the most natural thing in the world.

"What is it with you and spying?" I pause, because now a memory is resurfacing. "And come to think of it, whatever happened to you spying on your boss's wife?"

She shrugs. "I guess I realized she can't be that great if her husband is sleeping with me."

I give her a pleading look. "How much longer are you going to keep this up?"

"Oh no," she tut-tuts, "we're talking about *you* right now, not my crazy-as-shit relationship."

I consider her advice. "How is this going to work, exactly?"

"How do you mean?"

"Isn't Jared going to see me once I get there?"

"Just try to slip in unnoticed. You've taken me to a few of Maggie's parties, remember? No one seemed to know what the hell was going on after a while."

"True," I admit. "And what will happen if Jared sees me?"

"Eventually, you'll want him to see you. Tell him you wanted to surprise him. I'm sure he'll appreciate you trying to come, seeing as he drags you over the guilt coals whenever you don't."

I nod and set the mug on a coaster on her coffee table. "Okay. But what about Summer? Should I bring her?"

Jillian makes a face. "Definitely *not*. In fact..." Her eyes brighten. "Why don't you let me take care of her?"

I am dumbstruck. "Excuse me? *You* babysit?"

"Oh, please. I'm not that bad."

"But—I mean, have you ever taken care of a child in your life?"

"Had *you*?"

I grin. "*Touché*."

She stands up and holds out her hands. I take them and she heaves me off the couch. "Then it's settled. You will show up to that party looking your gorgeous self—"

"Gorgeous?" I arch an eyebrow. "I've barely squared at cute."

She rolls her eyes and continues, "I will take care of Autumn —"

"Her name's Summer."

"Summer, Winter, Fall. I knew it was a season. Anyway, I'll take care of her so you can have some 'you' time, then you call me on your way back with the joyous news that you and Jared are going to consummate your relationship. I'll be sure we skedaddle out of your place before things get too hot and heavy. I'll take her to a movie or something."

"That all sounds..." I hesitate, searching for the right word. I finally settle on the lame, "Nice."

Jillian folds her hands over her hips. "Why are you still looking like that? This idea's foolproof. You do the grand gesture of showing up. He'll finally admit to being madly in love with you and after-wards, you'll rack up a million orgasms!"

I burst out laughing, but inside I remember how awful my last grand gesture turned out—not to mention I'm still uncertain about my feelings towards him.

Jillian pouts at my expression. "You're still upset."

"It's just..." My voice trails and I sigh. "What if we're just not meant to be together?"

There's a brief silence. Then she whispers, "Do you want to just give up on him? You can, you know. Break up with him and take a few weeks off from men to heal..."

"No, no," I shake my head. "I love him."

"You're sure?"

"Yes," I say with genuine feeling. I do love Jared. What I fear is that he doesn't love me, and perhaps never has. If that's the case, we'll have to break up. And then I will have to admit that these past two years have all been a gigantic waste of my time.

Then I'll have to start all over again, which terrifies me even more.

Later that night, Summer watches silently as I apply eye shadow in the bathroom mirror. "Can I have some?" she asks at length.

I glance down at her and smile. Seeing her standing there puts a quiet stillness in my pounding heart. "Sure." I bend to dust a small amount of blue powder onto her lids.

"Ahhh," Jillian says when she sees us. "With that gorgeous Christmas tree over there, you look like you've stepped right out of a Norman Rockwell painting!"

"You really like it?" I ask. Summer and I puff up with pride.

"Ladies," Jillian says, bowing grandiosely, "you did great."

"High five!" Summer cries, slapping my hand excitedly and laughing.

Sobering with a last glance at the mirror, I return to Jillian. "Okay," I say, my hands clenching and unclenching. "What do you think?"

She gives me a critical look. "You want the truth?"

"No. I prefer you to lie to me." I actually do.

"You have got to stop with that blue eye shadow. Just *stop* it."

I cast a long look in the mirror. "But this is how I always look."

"And I always tell you that gem colors only work on children and blonde Hollywood starlets wearing feathered boas." She draws near to give me a full look-over. "And the black lipstick needs to go too. It makes you look like a corpse."

"It does not!" I exclaim. "And anyway, I think it makes my teeth look whiter."

"Like a *corpse*," Jillian emphasizes. "Nobody likes black lipstick, Kim. It's so gothic."

"Okay, okay. Anything else?"

She considers. "Maybe a different top. And pants."

"But I..." I'm about to say that I've had enough, that I like how I look, then realize that I never actually have. "What do you suggest?" I say instead, and Jillian beams.

She turns on the faucet, dampens a face towel, and says, "I thought you'd never ask."

"I think she looks nice," Summer pipes in, having watched our exchange with interest. I see the blue powder on her eyes and wonder if that color really only works on six-year-olds. And Hollywood starlets.

"Summer, I promise your aunt will look a thousand times better when I'm through with her." Jillian wrings the towel and scours my face free of any trace of makeup.

"I'm going to need a cigarette after this," I say, my heart hammering again.

"Oh, no, you won't," Jillian says with a firm shake of her head. "When was the last time you had one, anyway?"

"Last night," I say, but really I snuck one in a couple of hours ago.

"You so need to quit those nasty death-sticks." She spreads the moisturizer from her purse over my cheeks and forehead. "I bet you could quit cold turkey tonight if you wanted. My other friends were more addicted and managed to quit."

"What friends of yours smoked?"

"Just close your eyes," she orders, and the eye shadow brush executes small circles over my lids. "Remember Sharon? She used to smoke two packs a day. She's now been clean for over five years."

"I never knew that." In truth, I've always been a cigarette-and-beer kind of girl. I only really smoke when I get nervous or stressed —unfortunately, that's been pretty often lately.

"Open your eyes," she says, and I obey. "Okay, look at me. Seriously. Will you try to quit those things?"

I give a grudging nod. "Okay. I'll try."

"For real?"

"Yes."

"Great!" She takes up my purse, fishes inside, and promptly removes my carton of cigarettes.

"Right now?" Suddenly I'm craving one more badly than ever.

"Right now." She opens the box and promptly tosses the five remaining sticks into the toilet and flushes. I watch them spin and disappear with a sinking heart, before I remember the emergency box I keep under the cabinet. If only—

"And don't think I forgot these..." Jillian says, opening the cabinet and quickly finding my stash sitting on a set of hot curlers. She tears open the plastic and with another swift flush, my addiction is in the sewer. "So, how do you feel?"

"Okay," I say, although I'm already shaking, either from anticipation of tonight's party or the lack of nicotine, I don't know which. Probably both.

"Mommy says those are bad," Summer opines. She closes the lid of the toilet and sits on it with her legs bouncing. "*And* they make your breath smell bad."

"Thanks a lot!" I say, and both of them laugh.

"You should probably look into getting your teeth whitened too," Jillian suggests, then flashes a bright smile. "See these babies? Never touched a cigarette. Had them bleached two years ago. Now all I drink are clear diet colas and milky cappuccinos."

"And is it worth it?" I ask, wondering if my espresso maker will also have to go into the toilet.

"For the looks people give me when I smile? Absolutely. Now close your eyes. I want you to be dumb-struck when I finish."

In ten minutes she is done, but she rushes me from the bathroom before I can see my face and we peel apart my closet for something she deems "fashionably appropriate." We finally settle on a black boat-necked sweater, matching boots, and an old pair of jeans that settle right at my waist. "Because," she says sincerely, "those low risers are doing you no favors."

All this I obediently pull on, then Jillian hands Summer a brush and they both move to stand behind me. "Now your hair," Jillian says, clicking her tongue as she considers my unruly mop. "Okay. I've got it. Summer?"

"Yes?" my niece says, staring up at us with wide, expectant eyes.

"The brush, please." She extends her hand and Summer slides the brush to her as deftly as a nurse handing a physician a scalpel. After a moment, I realize what she's doing.

"You're pulling my hair *back*?" I raise my hands in self-defense.

Jillian immediately slaps them away. "You never show your face, Kim. Believe me, having it pulled back will highlight your best features."

"Which are?" I ask, not so much because I'm vain, but because I honestly couldn't name one.

"Well, your high cheekbones for one," Jillian says. "And your eyes. Very pretty."

"Really?"

"Really, sweetie. Okay, now don't move." And with a quick flourish, she is done. "You're ready," she says, then spritzes some of her perfume onto my hair and exposed shoulders. "Close your eyes."

"Do I have to?"

"Yes!" Jillian and Summer exclaim together.

I close my eyes as their hands guide me to the full-length mirror behind the bedroom door.

"Okay," Jillian murmurs. "Open them."

What I see is astonishing. Jillian has combed my hair back into an elegant French twist, with two small curls tumbling past my ears; my face looks fresh, with just a hint of rosy blush; my eyes look much larger with a soft beige power dusted on the lids and a chocolate brown shadow just over the crease. A nude lipstick and gloss make my usually rail-thin lips full and moist. And the sweater, boots, and jeans have harmonized into the first outfit I actually love on my body.

"Yay!" Summer chimes, hugging my leg. "You smell good, too!"

"What do you think?" Jillian asks.

"I..." Words fail me for a moment, but I quickly recover. "Oh my god. Thank you." I smile and for once I like the face that I see in the mirror. I may never be gorgeous, but right here, right now, I actually look *pretty*.

Jillian laughs and embraces me. Then, as if reading my thoughts, she says, "Oh, Kim. You were always pretty. You just covered yourself in so much crap that you couldn't see it."

Chapter Sixteen

I hear the music pounding from Maggie's apartment before I've even made it to the top of the stairs. Leave it to Maggie to throw a party reminiscent of high school. I grip my purse so tightly that my knuckles whiten.

Someone bounds past me on the landing, knocking me down a few steps. "Sorry!" the man says drunkenly, then snickers as he and a woman grasp lustily after each other and barely make it to their car.

I smooth back my now-stylish hair—giving a silent thanks to Jillian—and climb the rest of the stairs. My heart pounds and my stomach twists. Why am I so nervous? What do I think I'm going to find?

Maggie's door opens, and another couple spills out. A warm rush of air follows their exit and I manage a quick peek inside. I see Jared standing with his arms crossed, his usual Razorback cap slanted sideways, engaged in boisterous conversation with a couple I don't recognize.

My boots pick up and I'm inside. Pot smoke fills the small living room with a wispy, gray cloud and I fan myself a little as I ease forward. Strangers greet me and bump their way along, laughing. There's a keg with a huddled mass of people and a stereo playing techno.

I study Jared from across the room. He's chatting up a nice-looking couple. They grin and chuckle at his story. He starts up another one.

It's nothing. Completely harmless. Why had I worried? Lordy, I was going to give myself a heart attack.

I wipe my face and head over to surprise him, when a familiar woman rounds the corner and palms Jared's neck. It's an intimate gesture, reserved only for wives, girlfriends, and lovers. The back of his neck is *my* territory, and when I see my evil co-worker—now an evil bitch co-worker from hell—wrap her claws on the back of my boyfriend's neck, I shiver with shock and fury.

"Kim!" exclaims a voice on my left. "Wow! You look so different! I almost didn't recognize you."

"Hi, Maggie," I say, giving the hostess a fleeting smile before reverting to Jared, who now has his arm around Lisa's waist. *How the hell did this happen? How do they even know each other? What the—*

"Love what you did with your hair," Maggie says amicably as she sips her Budweiser. "Did you see Jared? He just came in a little while ago..."

"I see he didn't come alone," I reply darkly.

She follows my gaze, then issues a polite, "Oh. Well, they're just friends, Kim."

"Friends, huh?" Maggie is Jared's friend, so naturally she rises to his defense. "And how are they friends, exactly?"

"I'm not sure," she stammers, looking wildly about for someone else to talk to. "I thought they met through you—oh, Eddie! Hey!" And with that, she saunters off, leaving me alone.

My stomach cramps into a knot of rage. I'm usually the type

who cuts and runs when faced with adversity, but tonight something has shifted. I am not walking out of this party a coward.

Balling my fists, I march over to Jared and wrench Lisa's hand from his neck.

"Ouch!" she cries, staggering slightly on her heels as she turns to face me. She pales instantly. "Kim!"

"What?" Jared says, turning towards me. His face pulls into a look of surprised guilt, like a child caught with his hand in the proverbial cookie jar.

"Hi, sweetie," I say, forcing out the words. "I didn't know you knew Lisa so well."

"This isn't what it looks like." He takes a quick step away from my soon-to-be ex co-worker.

"Oh, no?"

"No, no." He flashes his disarming smiles, the one that used to melt my heart but now only hardens it. "She was just getting me a drink. We barely know each other."

"You two look pretty close to me."

"We're not," Jared assures. "Honestly, Kim, this is—"

"You asshole," I spit out. "You think you can screw around behind my back and get away with it? How long has this been going on?"

"Kim, it's—"

"Three months," Lisa says, folding her arms across her chest. She gives me a ruthless smile, and I see now that she truly hates me.

Jared glares at her. "Damn it, Lisa—"

"She should know, don't you think?" she says, her eyes bright as they bear down on me.

Standing there with the wild music pounding into my ears, staring at the two of them as drunks and near-drunks stumble past us, I realize I knew. I knew the whole time. I just didn't want to see it. Not again.

Because Jared has done this to me before. A year ago he admitted to having a one-night stand with some woman he met at a bar, but he was so tearfully sorry about the whole thing that I forgave him. In my weakness and desperation to keep him as a boyfriend, I forgave him. And I pushed it from my mind and have done well not to think about it since.

But I'm not playing the idiot a second time. I love Jared, but I realize now that I have to love myself more. "I'm leaving," I say, turning from them both.

Jared pales. He lurches forward to grip my hand with sudden violence. "*Don't*, Kim! Don't!"

I tear out of his iron grip and stare him down. "I'm leaving, Jared. And you can shove this relationship up your fucking ass."

And with that I leave, to the applause of two drunkards slumped against the wall who don't know any better.

Jared calls me twice on the way home, but I let it go to voicemail. I know it will just be more lies, more apologies, more promises that he will never do it again. I think about my mother, how much I wish she were here to talk to and comfort me. How I wish I could hold her again, breathe in the sweet scent of her hair. Even listen to one of her lectures about how I need to be careful with my heart, watch out for men who say one thing and do another. And my heart aches for both of them, for they are, in different ways, dead to me.

I somehow drag myself up the stairs to my apartment. My body weighs fifty pounds heavier, but I've not shed a tear. I just want to crawl into bed and sleep for a month and not have to worry about my life anymore.

"Hey!" Jillian says when I come in. "How did it—Oh my god! What happened?"

"Where's Summer?" I ask, lifting my purse from my shoulder as I collapse onto the couch.

"She seemed super tired, so I put her to sleep."

"Where?"

"In your bed. I was going to move her when you got back." Jillian quickly sits next to me. "What's wrong? What happened to you?"

I put my face in my hands and breathe out a sigh. "Jared and I broke up."

Jillian says nothing, only nods and massages my shoulder with her hand.

She looks so worried and sad that I almost hesitate telling her the next part. "He cheated on me," I manage at last. "With Lisa."

"Holy shit." Her eyes grow very wide. "Lisa, your *co-worker*?"

I nod.

"Holy *shit*."

I nod again.

"Was it a complete shock?" She shakes her head. "Stupid question, sorry. I mean, did you have any idea about this? Any clue about what was going on?"

"Yeah. I think I knew." I drag my legs into my chest and rest my chin on my knees. "I didn't tell you, but when I last went to his apartment, I heard these noises. And I thought..." I swallow hard as my throat closes in. "I thought he might be with someone else and I just walked away. I walked away rather than face what was really happening."

Jillian opens her arms. "Come here."

I let her embrace me as my stomach hollows. "I think I'm just going to go to bed."

"How about getting drunk?" Jillian throws her thumb towards my refrigerator. "I spotted some wine coolers in there. We can get hammered and whine about how men suck."

"No," I say, even though this is how I normally get over break ups. "No, that's okay. I really just want to turn in."

"Do you want me to stay over?"

I shake my head. "No, sweetie. What I want is to just be alone for a while."

"Okay." She follows me as I slowly stand. Then she says, "What are you going to do about work? Will you stay?"

"I don't know yet." I shrug. "All I know is that I'm definitely calling in sick tomorrow."

Jillian reaches forward to hug me again. "Call me for anything, okay? Seriously. I really wish you'd let me stay."

"It's nothing against you." I force myself to smile. "I just want to be alone."

"Okay." She shuffles to the door, then turns around and says, "I love you, Kim. If you need me, just call."

"Thanks," I say. "I love you, too. Goodnight."

I crawl into bed, holding my breath so I don't wake Summer. For a long time, I just stare up at the cracked ceiling, allowing the past two years with Jared to float over me. I remember all of our good times, mostly in the beginning. He and I waking up late in my bed on Sundays. Cooking pancakes with pan-fried bacon. Sipping coffee as I read *Parade* and he thumbed through the sports pages. Making love as we slowly discovered each other, me thrilled and disbelieving that such a handsome man could ever be interested in me. We'd watch movies curled up like a Twizzler on the couch, or take long walks outside if the weather was nice. Our birthdays and Christmases. Two anniversaries.

But things changed when I realized Jared wasn't getting serious, that he never said he loved me. I wouldn't be the first to say the Lword. I knew if a woman confessed her feelings first, she'd somehow lose the battle to the altar.

And when Jared first cheated on me, I stupidly thought his tears and seemingly endless apologies meant he'd finally realized how much he loved me. And I wanted that, at any cost. I rationalized the whole awful thing might have brought us closer together, that his guilt and my love would be enough for us.

I should have broken off our relationship right then. Maybe now I'd be with a man who understood, loved, and cherished me. That's what Mom wanted for me, and that's what I want for myself. I'm tired of these bullshit relationships that always end in tears and heartbreak. I want something *real*.

I roll onto my side and stare at my phone that's sitting on the nightstand. It flashes, announcing a new voicemail. Despite being bone-tired, I can't sleep. After a while, I slide from the bed and drag the phone into the living room.

"Kim, I am so, so sorry," comes Jared's recorded voice, followed by a heavy sigh. "I know you probably don't want to talk to me right now, but I am sorry. Lisa means nothing to me. She never did. It was just a dumb, stupid mistake. All I want is you."

Sure you do, I think. *Me and eventually another pretty skirt.*

"I saw how much I hurt you," he continues. "I'm so stupid to have fucked this up. Please don't give up on me, baby. Please don't. I..." His voice trails, and he takes in a steadying breath. "Kim, I love you."

My hand clutches at the phone. *Did he—? Wait. What'd he just say?*

"I love you, Kim," he says, more firmly now. "I should have said it a long time ago. I was just scared. You're my first serious relationship and I don't want to throw away everything we have over some dumb bitch. Please call me back. We can make this work if you just forgive me. I'm really sorry, Kim. Please find it in your heart to forgive me. I love you so much. I really do."

There's a click, then a mechanical, "End of messages."

I lower the phone to my lap. He said he loves me. He finally said he loves me. Two years together, and it takes sleeping with the Devil for him to realize it.

Why couldn't he have said it sooner? I'm like a silk dress doused in bleach. There's no fixing it.

I grimace and dial a number that I haven't willingly dialed in a long time.

"Hello?" says a soft voice, and this time the sound of my sister doesn't make me go cold all over. Instead, her familiar cadence reminds me of home and times long passed.

"It's me," I say, curling my legs into my chest. "It's Kim."

"Kim? Is everything okay?" Dena's motherly concern's suddenly understandable to me. "Is everything okay? Has something happened since this afternoon? Is—"

"Everything's fine," I assure her. "Summer's doing great."

"Oh. Oh, good." After a pause, she asks in a suspicious voice, "Are you okay? You sound weird."

I take in a shallow breath. "It's been a rough night. I..." I stop, swallow hard, then finish the sentence, "I broke up with Jared."

"Oh, honey. What happened?"

A cramp seizes my stomach. *I can't hide the truth anymore.* "He cheated on me."

There's a brief silence. "Oh, *honey.*"

"It's happened before," I say in a rush. "And I forgave him. This time—"

"You're throwing him to the curb," Dena finishes. "Like the trash he is."

"Yeah. I think so." I wipe my nose with the back of my hand. "He said he loves me. Just now. On my voicemail."

"Kim..." she begins, and I know she's about to give me a lecture.

"No, no," I say quickly before she can start. "I'm not taking him back. I just need to think about things. How I got here and why I stayed so long."

"Is there anything I can do?"

"There is," I pause. "Can we talk about Mom?"

Dena says nothing. For a moment, I worry the line's disconnected. Then, in a small, firm tone, she says, "You know I don't like to talk about her."

"Please? I just miss her so much. I remember how we'd play in our old backyard and how she'd tickle us to make us laugh."

"She was pretty crazy," Dena says, and I can tell she's smiling.

"I'm starting..." My eyes well with tears. I draw a steadying breath. "I'm forgetting things. Like what she smelled like. I know she smelled sweet, but not what it was, exactly. Or how her skin felt. Do you remember?"

Dena quiets for a long time. I tense up, worried I'd gone too far. At last, she says, "It was a long time ago."

"I know. It's just—I wish we'd had more time with her. The accident..."

"Please, Kim. I know you're upset, but I don't want to talk about this, especially on vacation. Okay?"

All the fight goes out of me. "Okay. Fine."

"I'm sorry. It's just..." She sighs.

"What?"

"This vacation hasn't exactly been what I hoped it'd be."

"What do you mean?" I picture her and her perfect husband skiing the slopes, enjoying a four hundred dollar bottle of champagne in a Jacuzzi, followed by passionate sex on a polar bear rug.

"I thought—" She stops. Breathes hard. "I have to go. Can I talk to you later?"

"Sure. Is everything okay?"

"It's fine. Got to go. Bye."

I stare at the dead phone in my shaking hand. What's wrong with her? Had something happened?

As I make my way back to bed and Summer's slumbering form, I wonder if maybe my sister's marriage isn't as perfect as I thought.

Just as I settle in, my phone blinks and Jared's name flashes across the screen. I ignore it and curl into Summer, whose soft breath blooms against my chest. Gradually, I fall asleep.

In my dream, my mother's young and beautiful. She holds me even as my hot tears soak the front of her blouse. "It's okay," she murmurs, stroking my hair. "Everything'll be all right."

I grip her almost to the point of pain. "I miss you so much, Mami."

"I miss you too."

"I miss you more."

"Impossible, my sweetheart."

"Oh, Mami. I'm so alone."

"You're not alone, Kimmy."

All my fear and doused hope explode in a tempest. "I *am* alone, Mami. I'm all alone in this world!"

"You'll always have me," she whispers, kissing my wet cheek. "And there are others..."

"What others?" I ask, trying to grip her tighter.

But all I hold is empty air.

Chapter Seventeen

SATURDAY, JUNE 14, 1997

The final bridesmaid turns the corner and I hear Dena take a sharp intake of breath, which is difficult from the rigid stays in her bodice.

"You okay?" I ask, awkwardly clutching the duchess satin of her train in my hands.

She doesn't look at me, but calls over her shoulder, "I'm fine. It's just nerves." She wipes nonexistent dust from her capped sleeves. She looks so beautiful, even if her enormous ball gown threatens to consume her. There is the monarch train—splayed between my hands—and the ten-foot veil, as well as the enormous Swarovski crystal tiara that sparkles high above her forehead. Jonathan's parents, a pair of Wall Street retirees, did well in the stock market this year and offered to pay for everything, down to my cerise attendant's attire.

The music pauses. Dena shifts her pink calla lily bouquet to the opposite hand. The videographer comes round, grapples with his shoulder camera, and zooms in on Dena's face. I wonder what she looks like just then. Is she happy? Nervous? Scared? As a nineteen-year-old dateless wonder, I can't imagine being married.

"Canon in D" starts on the organ. Dena steps forward and I follow, letting the train spool out until it falls between us like a white river. Dena walks alone, despite her future father-in-law's offer to escort her. "It was supposed to be Dad," she told me once. "So now it's just me."

The pews groan as everyone rises. I give a final fluff to the train before stepping back. The music stops again, and then Felix Mendelssohn's "Wedding March" echoes into the rafters.

Dena—proud, alone, and confident—strides with a stately air up the aisle.

I slip into my seat and think of Mom. In three days it'll be the year anniversary of her death. My throat tightens. Hot tears track down my temples. I lower my head and wipe my eyes, forcing a smile so that I can pretend the tears are ones of happiness for my sister.

Dena and Jonathan bow their heads in prayer. Mom would have been so happy to see this. I wonder if Dena is thinking of Mom right now, wishing she were here to look on, to give advice and praise. I want to talk about Mom so often, but I know this is a closed subject. I'm done trying to push her, because Dena will simply give me a dark look and walk away.

It is no surprise then that I am Dena's attendant instead of a bridesmaid. We haven't been friends for a long time, even before Mom's death. It would have felt false standing up there beside her. When she asked me to be her attendant—which I suspected then and know now was only out of pity—I offered no resistance. I wasn't a part of her life. And I probably will never be again.

After a lengthy mass, the priest closes his enormous Bible and proclaims, "You may now kiss your bride!"

Dena wraps her arms around Jonathan's broad shoulders, giving herself entirely to the kiss. My heart grips. I don't have anyone like that in my life, and it's an aching void that has become as familiar as my own skin.

The trumpeter blares his horn and Dena and Jonathan turn to thunderous applause. I follow everyone outside, filling my hands with proffered pink rose petals and tossing them at the happy couple as they laugh and prance outside the church. Jonathan helps her into the white limousine and they wave goodbye. The limo pulls away toward the reception and I sigh and re-shoulder my purse, then walk alone to my awaiting car.

I catch my reflection in the dark glass of the driver's door. I should be happy for my sister. But all I feel is numb. My only sibling is moving to the east coast and may never return. Both of our parents are dead. I have no other family, no boyfriend, not even a close girlfriend.

Maybe this will change. But right now, I am truly alone.

Chapter Eighteen

TUESDAY, DECEMBER 20, 2005

"Okay, now just slide your feet in the stirrups, lean back, and try to relax," instructs Heather, the nurse practitioner, smiling sweetly as she watches me struggle in my paper nightgown.

I want to ask why my usual doctor isn't doing the Pap smear, but this nurse hasn't let me get a word in edge-wise. Besides, I'm lucky my appointment didn't get canceled from all the women tapping their feet in the waiting room. I've never seen a space so full of people eager to get something over with. When another nurse asked for my urine sample, she had me scrawl my name onto a paper cup and deposit it into a little silver window—where four other cups with four other black signatures were already waiting. It grossed me out so much that I washed my hands about a million times, gloving my hand in a paper towel so that I could open the bathroom door without actually touching it.

"You looking forward to Christmas?" my nurse asks, basting a frighteningly long Q-tip with K-Y jelly.

"I guess," I say, trying to sound non-committal, hoping she won't keep talking to me.

"Because I love Christmas. It's my favorite holiday of the year. The presents, the tree, all the chocolate and cookies. Yes, it's my favorite holiday by far." She reminds me of Mrs. Claus: she's short and plump with over-rouged cheeks and has a jolly demeanor. I just wish she would stop talking and let me wallow in self-pity. "I used to make stockings for all my grandchildren, but I have some minor arthritis that makes it difficult to work the needles."

Arthritis? I watch her balance the Q-tip in a pudgy hand and tense up, which she immediately chastises.

"*Relax*. Now, who do you spend Christmas with?" She places a warm hand on my outer thigh and directs me to scoot down further.

"Um, usually with some friends." I spread my legs and wince as an icy, unforgiving instrument pushes inside me and winds up like a toy.

"Just friends?" Nurse Heather asks in surprise. "What about your family?"

"My dad died when I was a kid, and then my mom passed when I was in high school." I know it's wrong, but I enjoy watching some of the nurse's Christmas cheer evaporate.

"Oh." She pauses, and a brief sadness passes over her face, but then she recovers. "Well, it's good you have friends then. Are you married?"

"No," I say, growing weary. "But I did just break up with the man I thought I was going to marry. Does that count for anything?"

She clears her throat. "This will only take a moment."

The Q-tip scrapes inside. My eyes water.

"Relax, honey. Goodness, you're as tight as a drum. Just relax —"

"I *am* relaxed!" I snap, immediately regretting my outburst. "Sorry. It's just been a very rough week."

"That's okay. Just a little more—there!" She removes the Q-tip and slides another in.

I roll my head, crinkling the white butcher paper. "How much more of this?"

"Just a moment more. You know I'm glad that you scheduled this. It's not good to wait three years for a Pap smear. At your age, you should watch for irregularities."

In truth, I would have never scheduled this stupid appointment had my new insurance company not required a physical. "I know. That's why I'm here."

"Very good," she says, then stands and paces to the sink, where she deposits the Q-tips into two glass cylinders. I watch her grease her right hand with more lubricating jelly. "Now I need to check your ovaries and uterus. Try to relax."

I roll my head back and forth and try thinking pleasant thoughts. But all I can think of is Jared and all his unreturned calls. And there's Dena, who's acting super weird and not telling me why. I've taken four sick days because I can't face my evil co-worker. Do I return to the office? Quit? If I quit, what next? And good grief, is Christmas just five days away?

"You're tensing up again. Please, Ms. Kincaid, try to relax or this may hurt."

"I'm trying," I say, closing my eyes and taking a few steadying breaths. As the nurse eases her hand into me, I can't help thinking that this will probably be the last bit of action I'll see for a long time, if not forever. I almost want to laugh.

"Good!" She stands and snaps off her gloves. "I'll have these tests run, and you should hear from us in a few days if there's anything unusual. Okay?"

"Sure." I slide off the paper and quickly hike up my panties.

"Do you have any questions?" she asks, still cheery.

"No."

"None at all?"

"Nope."

"Okay, sweetie. Well, you have a great Christmas." She drops a piece of paper on the examining table. "Just bring that and the one you got from your physical to the front when you're done. Have a fabulous afternoon!" And with that, she steps behind a broad curtain, opens the door, and discreetly closes it behind her.

My phone rings and an unfamiliar number flashes on the screen. I wonder if it's Jared calling from someone else's line since I've been screening his calls. Then, figuring Jared would never be that clever—or desperate—I pick up on the third ring. "Hello?"

"May I speak to Ms. Kincaid?" calls a high-pitched voice.

"Speaking," I say in my office tone. "Who's calling?"

"This is Bethany from Ben & Jerri's Day Care Center."

I imagine Summer on a stretcher being wheeled into a hospital. "Oh my god. Is everything okay?"

"Everything's fine. Summer just has a minor stomach bug, and we thought it'd be best if you took her home for the day."

"Is it serious?"

"No, Ma'am. No fever or vomiting. But she says she's nauseated. We usually find it best for them to be in the comfort of their own home."

Home away from home, I think, already wrestling on my jeans. "That's fine. I'm on my way to pick her up now."

"Aunt Kim!" Summer calls, rushing to embrace my legs. "I missed you!"

"Aww, I missed you too, kiddo." I stroke her head affectionately. "How are you feeling?"

"A lot better," she says, taking my hand as we make our way to the car. Then, once we're safely out of earshot, she looks up at me and says, "I really just wanted to be with you."

Ha! The little faker. I probably would have pulled the same stunt at her age, too. "You couldn't have picked a better time," I say, reflecting on my lack of a job, boyfriend, or any other tie-up most women my age grapple with. "How do you feel about some Christmas shopping?"

"Yes!" she cheers. "Let's go! Let's go!"

"Okay, but we can't spend too much. 'Tis the season to be frugal, at least with your aunt."

"I don't care!" she exclaims. "I'm just happy I don't have to make any more Play-dough castles."

The mall looks ready to collapse from all the post-Thanksgiving and pre-December 24th holiday shoppers. Summer is ecstatic since she—like her mother—thrives among large groups of people. I have a different sort of reaction, bordering on agoraphobia. "Let's sit down," I say, eyeing a bench that's just opened up.

"Can I have a pretzel?" she asks.

"Sure." I dig into my wallet and hand her five dollars. "Go nuts."

She skips away to the pretzel stand and I watch her from a few feet away. Even though she can't quite reach the counter, she makes her desire known and soon she's back with change and a piping-hot cinnamon pretzel.

"Want some?" she offers, very graciously, for a six-year-old.

"Don't mind if I do." My small bite triggers a memory. I smile and say, "Did you know that when your mother and I went out with your grandmother, she would say to us in this crazy British accent, 'Ello, Dena! 'Ello, Kimmy! How do you do?'"

Summer laughs, like I always used to do. "Why would she talk like that?"

"I don't know." I peel off another piece of pretzel. "It was just something we did every morning. And after we'd reply, she'd always say, 'I do fine, how do you?'" I chuckle.

"What was she like?" Summer asks, wiping her sticky mouth with the back of her hand.

"Well, what does your mom say about her?"

"Not much," she admits, her smile fading. "Daddy doesn't like Mom talking about her."

Sudden anger flares inside me. *How dare Jonathan stifle our mother's memory!* "Why is that?" I ask as gently as possible.

"Because talking about her always makes Mom sad." Summer puts the pretzel in her napkined lap and sighs. "She cries sometimes. And that makes me sad, too."

"Oh." I feebly hold the piece of pretzel in my hand, consider tossing it, and then finally drop it in my mouth. "Well, your grandmother was an extraordinary woman. She raised your mom and me by herself for a long time."

"What did she look like?"

I wrap my arm around Summer and draw her closer. "Well, she was very kind and very beautiful. She had short blonde hair that was gold in the sun, bright blue eyes, and always smelled like vanilla and lemons."

"Why did she smell like that?" Summer asks, her eyes bright with interest.

"Because she loved cleaning with anything labeled lemon or vanilla-scented." I laugh. "She kept our small house so clean and orderly that it looked so much better than it probably was. I used to clean as much as she did, before my boy—*ex*-boyfriend—came along."

"I like to clean too!" Summer says. "Our house is very clean."

"I bet." I imagine a throng of cleaning women sweeping through Dena's mansion bi-weekly. "Okay, kiddo. How about we look at some clothes for yours truly and then see what's at the toy store?"

"Okay!" She stands and deposits her trash in a wastebasket nearby.

We spot a Petite Sophisticate at the end of the mall and Summer helps me peruse its various racks of business attire. So much is on sale that my mind is spinning. I cannot remember the last time I shopped for clothes. I'm also wondering if I should buy anything since I may very well be out of a job soon (such frugal habits have helped me save over thirty percent of my paycheck). Then again, a few hundred dollars wouldn't put a crushing blow into my savings, and it *would* make me feel better. As I fill my arms with jackets and pants and camisoles, a saleswoman offers to set up a room for us, which I gratefully accept.

It's as I'm slipping on a smart red suit jacket that my mobile rings in my purse. "Summer?" I say, struggling with the buttons. "Can you get my phone?"

She fishes through my purse and hands it to me.

I see the name and flip it open. "Hey, Jillian. What's up?"

"Did I just see you duck into a changing room?" she asks, sounding thrilled.

"Oh my god! Are you in the mall, too?"

"Great! I'll be there in a sec!" She hangs up and I grin and return the phone to Summer.

A moment later there comes a knock on my door and I open it, still only half-dressed. "What are you doing here?"

"Shopping on my lunch hour." Jillian sashays inside and waves to Summer. "You're still calling in sick, I see."

"I can't really face Lisa right now." I suck in my stomach so that I can zip up the skirt. "Okay," I say, wanting to change the subject, "what do you think?"

They both give me a disapproving look.

"What?" I ask, pouting.

"Red is just not your color," Jillian says. "And anyway, if you're looking for something professional to wear at work, I suggest something in black, navy, or beige."

"But those colors are so boring."

"Boring," she says, putting up an instructive finger, "but *professional*. Trust me." She exits the dressing room and comes back with two identical triacetate suits, one in black and the other in navy. "Are you still a size ten?"

"Yes," I admit, giving her petite frame an envious glance.

"Okay. Here." She takes the black blazer from its hanger and hands it to me. "Let's make sure the shoulders fit right and that the waist's tapered. Also, the skirt should fall just above your knees."

"How do you know all this?" I ask, working the buttons.

"I've picked stuff up over the years. Before I was first interviewed, I bought a book on how to dress for success and it really helped. I'm certain that's why they chose me over the other applicants."

"Okay," I say, dropping my hands. "What do you think?"

They nod approvingly. Summer says, "You look like Mom!"

"I wish," I say, turning to Jillian. "And you?"

"You look great." She's grinning with pride. "And with your hair pulled back—now, Kim," she says, seeing my face, "you know you look good that way."

"So you keep telling me." I sigh. "I guess I'll just have to get used to it."

"So why are you trying these on?" Jillian asks, accepting the blazer and passing over the navy one. "You don't have to wear these as a secretary."

"I'm thinking of changing jobs," I murmur, still terrified by this idea.

Her eyes widen. "Really? Like what?"

"Well…" my voice trails. *Should I tell her?*

"What, Kim?" She's eyeing me with renewed interest.

"I'm thinking of going to college," I say at last, because it's something I've thought about ever since that horrible night with Jared. A chance for a clean start. And—*maybe*—a better future.

"Oh, Kim!" Jillian's smile is humongous. "That's *great*! Good for you. What are you thinking of majoring in?"

"I don't know yet. But I see so many non-traditional students on campus that it gives me hope I can do it too. I'll try to find some part-time work. Someplace nice where I could wear these suits."

"Of course," Jillian says, nodding seriously.

"And I could live off my savings and take loans for the rest." I'm out of breath. "What do you think?"

"I think it's a fabulous idea. I bet you're even eligible for scholarships."

"Oh, I don't know," I say doubtfully. "I didn't make great grades in high school. I barely scraped by."

"But they offer so much now and there's funding *specifically* for non-traditionals. I think you should at least look into it. It can't hurt, right?"

"Right," I say, but I'm still hesitant. "Just remember, it's still just an idea. It hasn't happened yet. And if I decide to do it, it'll probably take me a million years to finish."

She smiles. "I'm really proud of you for even considering this. It's really great."

"Thanks." I wonder if I'll actually go through with it. I've always been a dreamer, but I've never made a single dream real. Grimacing, I zip up the skirt and turn around. "Okay. How about this one?"

❄

I end up purchasing both the navy and black suits at one hundred and twenty dollars each, which I'm assured is a bargain. Once Jillian expertly pulls back my hair and locates the perfect white camisole to go underneath the blazers and two-inch pumps, I spontaneously decide to wear the black suit around the mall. I lift my chin as I swing my shopping bags in one hand and hold Summer's hand with the other. I look like a woman who has her life together, and even though that may not be the case, at least I can pretend.

We're passing a MAC counter when Jillian suddenly cries, "Stop!"

Summer and I both jump, but we obediently halt. "What is it?" I ask, following her gaze.

"They're offering free makeovers!" Jillian's beaming. "Okay, here. Sit down and I'll get the technician." And off she flies as I set down my bags and gratefully take a seat.

"How are you doing, Summer?" I smile down at her as she peers into the glowing makeup cabinets.

"This is fun." She glances up at me. "You look really nice."

"Thanks," I say, slightly unnerved by the compliments.

Jillian returns with a woman in a white lab coat. "Okay," Jillian says. "She says we made it just in time."

"What colors do you like?" the woman asks, peering at my face with fierce scrutiny.

"Um, well..." I look at Jillian. "Why don't you tell her? You seem to know more about it than I do."

"Gladly," she says, turning to the beautician. And for a second time in a week, my face has a total beauty overhaul (under Jillian's careful supervision, of course).

By the time the mirror's turned to me, I expect a clown to be staring back for all the layered makeup. Instead, my reflection shows a smart, sophisticated, and moderately attractive woman. In my new suit, I look like a leader. I look like the person I've always wanted to be.

"Thank you," I say, still unable to process my reflection. I wish we'd brought a camera, which is huge, because I normally hate being photographed.

"Okay, then!" Jillian turns to the beautician. "I'd like to purchase every item you used on my friend here today."

"You like it that much, huh?" I say with a grin.

Jillian laughs. "I sure did. But this is for *you*. This is your Christmas present."

I'm taken aback, knowing this will cost well over our fifty-dollar Christmas limit. "Oh, Jillian. You can't! It's too much!"

But Jillian gives a determined shake of her head. "No way. You've needed some proper makeup for a long time. Plus, I consider it an honor shepherding you towards a new career."

I sway on my heels. I hate her spending so much on me, especially when I can never match such generosity. "Are you sure?"

"Please." She slides her crisp silver credit card across the counter. "I'm sure. What's a best friend for?"

My ears burn when I hear the astronomical price, so I thank Jillian profusely as we make our way through the store.

"Enough, already!" she insists, laughing. "Summer, what do you think of your aunt's new look?"

"It's amazing!"

"You two are nuts," I say with a jubilant smile. This day couldn't get any better.

It's at that moment that we make a turn and I nearly collide with Rachel Davis, my arch nemesis from high school. She still carries her Gucci purse, but now has two red-faced boys and—I'm assuming—a nanny in tow. She doesn't look half as put together as when I saw her at the office.

"*Excuse* me," she snaps, about to push past.

She doesn't recognize me, I think, realizing that Rachel isn't intimating now that I'm not catering to her from behind a desk. Pulling myself to my full height, I say, "Hello, Rachel."

Rachel stops to look at me. Her eyes narrow, but there is no recognition in them. "Yes? Do I know you?" One child puts the other in a headlock, and the nanny pulls both boys aside to reprimand them.

"Yes," I say, smiling with my newfound confidence. "I'm Kim Kincaid. Remember me?"

Her eyes scan my body as her grin turns icy. "Yes. I didn't recognize you all goosed up. I didn't realize they expected secretaries to dress professionally."

Jillian opens her mouth to make a heated retort when I say, "What do you *do*, Rachel?" I had wanted to say this when I'd seen her those many days ago, but had not had the courage.

She hesitates and for a moment looks at a loss. But she recovers quickly, haughty annoyance edging her tone. "Well, I don't have a career *per se*, but I—"

"So you don't have one," I finish for her.

"No. I'm a *mother*. And I am an active member of the PTA, among other organizations—"

"So, you're a housewife." I pointedly look at the woman struggling with her unruly children. "With a nanny."

Rachel's lips curl. "Sasha only helps when I'm busy. And I really don't have time for this."

As she turns to go, I grasp her shoulder and force her around. "You're rotten," I spit out, tightening my grip. "You lived to make my life miserable, even after my mother died. You act like you're better than everyone else, but you're not. At least I'm making something of myself! What are you doing? You don't know struggle. You don't know loss. You're mean and cruel and nothing more than a callous snob who doesn't know people are laughing at her!"

I drop my hands and Rachel staggers back.

"With a Gucci rip-off!" Jillian adds gleefully.

I snatch Summer's hand. "Let's go."

We only make a few steps before Rachel exclaims, "You—you *bitch!*"

"That's the best you can think of?" Jillian calls over her shoulder as I pick up the pace.

"She said the B-word," Summer says in surprised tones.

"That's because she doesn't have your aunt's vocabulary," Jillian explains.

I'm shaking from the confrontation that's been building up for years. Unseen shackles fall away with each breath. Once we turn the corner and officially put the Queen of Snobs behind us, I say, "Was her purse really a fake?"

Jillian grins. "*Totally.* In fact, I'd say everything about that woman is fake. Good job standing up to her. I'd always hoped we'd cross paths with you looking your gorgeous self."

"I'm not anywhere near gorgeous," I correct her. "But at least I feel good about myself. And that's all I've ever wanted."

Chapter Nineteen

"I still can't believe you told that bitch off!" Jillian says as we climb the stairs to my apartment.

"*Jillian!*" I gesture towards Summer, who's shaking her head disapprovingly at both of us.

"Sorry, kid," Jillian says. "Apparently, I need to think of some better synonyms. How about stupid-head?"

"Yeah!" Summer agrees. "And doo-doo head!"

"Actually, I'd say that one fits her to a T." Jillian musses my niece's hair. "Good job."

"Hi, Kim!" calls a voice from the landing.

"Hi, Alice," I say with a smile, loving how easily smiles are suddenly coming to me. I recognize the man she's with as the one who helped Summer and me set up our Christmas tree. "How are you?"

"I'm fine." She moves a little so the five of us can stand together. "Don't you look nice! I love that suit."

"Thanks." I'm unable to stop the blush that rises to my cheeks.

"And how are you doing, Summer?" Alice asks her.

"Good," she says, smiling politely.

"No more bad nights, I take it?" she asks me.

"Thank goodness, no." Alice nods approvingly and I sneak a quick glance at Brandon, wondering how they know each other. I hope they're not dating. "She's been pretty good lately. Where are your boys?"

"With their father, which is nice because I needed a break to work on my apartment." She extends her hand to Jillian. "Hi, I'm Alice Varady. I live next door to Kim."

"That's amazing that you two know each other," Jillian says, shaking the proffered hand. "I've had the same neighbors for six years and I don't so much as know their first names."

After we laugh, Alice nods at the man standing alongside. "This is my brother, Brandon Williams."

He smiles at me. "We've actually met."

"Yes!" I say, a little too excitedly. "You helped us set up our Christmas tree."

"We put up the ornaments!" Summer announces. "You should see it. It's really nice."

"Thanks for your help again," I tell him.

"Not a problem," Brandon replies, smiling. "I'm glad I could help."

"And are you married?" Jillian asks him abruptly.

"Uh, no," he says with an amused laugh.

Jillian nods, as if taking mental notes. "So, you're just visiting your sister?"

"Yep. I'm helping her move out in a few days."

"You're moving?" I say to Alice, who nods. "That's too bad."

"You'll have to come visit my new place. It's only a few minutes from here. And bring Summer," she adds with a grin.

"Oh, I almost forgot." I root through my wallet and finally produce her supermarket discount card. "Thanks again for this."

"Any time." She pockets it. "So, what are you guys doing tonight? Brandon and I were just heading out to dinner."

Brandon looks at me and says, "Would you like to join us?"

I shake my head. "We actually just got back and I'm pretty exhausted. And I'm on a budget."

"I see." Brandon laughs, pointedly eyeing my two bursting shopping bags.

"Starting now," I amend.

"You sure?" Alice presses.

I nod. "Some other time. But thanks for the invite."

"Well, you guys have a good night." Brandon shakes our hands again. "Great to see you, Kim. Bye Summer." And the two of them walk down the stairs, talking animatedly.

"He seems nice," Jillian says once we're inside my apartment.

"Yeah, he does." I sit down on the couch.

"*And* cute."

"I guess." I look up at her and suddenly realize the meaning behind her pointed remarks. "Oh, are you interested in him?"

"No, no," Jillian says, sitting next to me. "He's perfect for *you*."

"Me?" I ask, feigning disinterest. "What are you talking about?"

"Come on. He's cute, funny, charming, *obviously* a nice guy. He's exactly what you need."

I put up my hands. "I'm not starting a new relationship on the heels of a two-year one. I need time for myself, okay?"

"Okay, okay. I'm just saying that he's into you."

I roll my eyes. "Please."

"Seriously. I saw him checking you out." She pokes me playfully in the shoulder. "Little Ms. Hot-to-Trot."

"I like him," Summer chirps as she plays with her Barbies on the carpet. "He's nice."

"You've said that before," I remind her. "And no. I'm not going after him, okay? I seriously need some time just to be *me*."

"All right," Jillian says with a sigh. "Sorry." Then, after a moment, "So you're not at *all* attracted to him? Because I could have sworn there was something going on between you two—"

"No! Oh my god, Jillian. You don't give up."

"It's my forte." She grins proudly. "So, what do we do now?"

"First, I'm going to change out of this before my luck runs out and I ruin it." I stand and head into the bedroom.

When I return in some exercise pants and an oversized sweatshirt, Jillian says, "So now what?"

"I don't know." I join her on the couch and stare off into the distance. Summer is still playing on the carpet, so I lower my voice so that just Jillian can hear. "It's just so hard. I can't believe it's really over between Jared and me. And after all that time together."

"I can only imagine." Jillian herself has only sustained two one-year relationships, with the rest being a series of casual ones. "Do you know what I do after a breakup?"

I try to remember, but can't. "What?"

"First, we need a big box." Spotting one next to my garbage can, she marches over and opens it. "Perfect."

"What do you do with it?"

"We find all the stuff that even remotely reminds you of your ex, put it in the box, and have a ritual burial."

"You seriously do this every time you break up with someone?"

"Absolutely," she says, and then glances about. Seeing a picture of Jared and me on the kitchen counter, she picks up the offending frame and announces, "Photographs should be the first to go."

"But I look cute in that picture!" I protest, not because I actually do, but because I don't want to throw away all these memories. *Not just yet.*

"Then you simply cut him out of it." She pantomimes a pair of scissors. "Snip, snip."

"Can we start with something easier?"

"Like what?"

I shrug helplessly.

She looks around, then declares, "Bathroom!" and stomps off. She returns brandishing his toothbrush, aftershave balm, and razor. "Perfect start."

"Okay." I never liked how he cluttered my bathroom. I'd told him about a million times to stop spitting all over the mirror and to keep the cap on his toothpaste—both of which never, ever happened. "Those can go. And whatever else of his you find in there, I guess."

"Excellent. Let's go." She drags me in and we methodically deposit an assortment of utilities into the rapidly filling box. Meanwhile, Summer transitions her playtime into my bedroom, singing an unknown melody. I take up a wad of paper towels and a spray cleaner and scrub the sink and the inside of the tub. Then I turn my attack to every spot and smudge on the mirror, faucets, and handles. I usually do this on Sunday, to keep the chaos from reverting. Of course, Jared never once helped me. Maybe now order will actually stick.

After a few minutes, I glance at Jillian. "So, how are you and Adam doing?"

"As good as can be expected." She gives a faint shrug. "I don't know."

"What do you mean?"

She's squatting beside the cabinet underneath the sink, searching for anything masculine. "Well, he has this purposeful space drawn up between us that's getting to me. It's as if he doesn't want to have too many feelings or else it could jeopardize his relationship at home."

"I don't think that's too unusual." I wet a paper towel, wring out the excess water, and start on the floor. "Maybe you're not the first one he's cheated on his wife with."

"I know," she says ruefully. "I just feel myself falling for him every day and..." Her voice trails and she's silent for a moment. "And it's just getting harder to keep it purely physical, you know?"

"That comes with intimacy, Jillian. You can't expect to keep all emotions under lock and key."

"I guess not." She pauses. "But you loved Jared, right?"

I start a little at the sudden shift in topic. "Yes. Of course."

"And how did you know?"

I consider this for a few moments. "I don't know how. Maybe I sensed it. I see now that my questioning my love for him wasn't so much that I didn't love him, but that I feared he didn't feel the same."

Jillian nods, her expression solemn. "I think that's what's happening to me. I feel like I love him, but still wrestle with doubt. I just don't know what's going to happen."

"So, why did you put yourself in this position?" I don't want to push her, but I need to know.

"At first it was just about sex, which I thought wouldn't last very long. But then it grew into this *thing*. And now my job's tied in it and it's getting very complicated. I've been shitting where I eat." She rolls her eyes. "I admit it wasn't the smartest thing to do."

"No, it wasn't. But you'll get through this. Everything has to end at some point, right?"

She cocks a suspicious eyebrow. "Who are you? How did you get so wise?"

"Believe me, it wasn't by choice. Being with Jared actually taught me a few things."

"Oh?" she says doubtfully. "Like what?"

I finish the small patch of linoleum between the tub and sink and toss the soiled paper into the box by the door. "That I shouldn't let life pass me by. And that I shouldn't be scared to ask for what I want. And to have the courage to speak up when I know some-thing's wrong."

"All very important things." She follows my paper towel with a bottle of Jared's deodorant, her third deodorant discovery since opening my lower cabinets. I suddenly wonder how much crap Jared has amassed all over my home, relieved to see the box filling with his pollutants. Jillian has herself nearly wedged inside the cabinet when she says, "I wonder what being with Adam will teach me?"

"Hopefully something good," I call to her. *How* are *things going to turn out for us?*

Soon enough, we've purged any physical sign of my ex. A knot releases in my chest as I gaze at my pristine bathroom. "It's weird."

"What's weird?"

"I didn't know he'd made such a mess of things."

"Of your life, honey." Jillian hauls the box into her arms. "Okay. Where to next?"

Later that night, after Jillian heads home, Summer is splashing in the tub, completely soaking the front of my shirt. "Hey!" I exclaim, instinctively splashing her back. I'd filled the tub with a raspberry-scented bubble bath and covered Summer in a foamy mass of bubbles. She laughs, thinking the whole thing is absolutely hilarious.

"Look, Aunt Kim!" she says, scooping up the bubbles and spreading some along her chin. She giggles hysterically. "I have a beard!"

"I see that." I pour some shampoo into my hands and work it into a lather. "Okay, stay still for a sec." I massage her head and Summer closes her eyes and hums with pleasure. "Okay," I say at length. "Lean back." She does, and I part the bubbles and pour some water from the faucet over her head until it's clean.

I am so happy at this moment, happier than I've been in years. Even though I don't know what my future holds, at least I have my niece—whom I love and who loves me back—and we'll always have each other. It's a comforting feeling, having a family.

"I hear something," Summer says, opening her eyes and looking over my shoulder.

"What?" I strain to listen. And then I hear it: a faint knock. "Stay here," I say, quickly rinsing my hands in the sink and walking to the door. Suspecting it's Jared come to beg my forgiveness, I hesitantly ask, "Who's there?"

"It's me," comes a small, defeated voice. "Dena."

Chapter Twenty

Mom died three days ago. I still can't believe it. I told several people what happened, but it still feels like I'm speaking about somebody else's life. Surely it cannot be mine.

They told me Mom's car crashed into a tree, and she died on the way to the hospital. It was all very sudden. The doctors say she endured little pain. A dark part of me wishes she'd held on longer so I could see her. Maybe say goodbye. But then I think I probably would've done nothing but sob the whole time and ruined whatever experience death is supposed to be. So perhaps it's better this way.

I don't know.

I'm on my way to the funeral and I don't know what to say to Dena once I get there. My father is the only other person who has died in our family, but it was so long ago that I wonder what the proper feelings should be, how I should react to all of this. There's a hardening in my heart that I can't fully explain. It's heavy as lead. I worry the best part of me died along with my mother.

Nightmares plague me. I see myself in the passenger seat with Mom, slamming into a giant oak tree. Crashing through the glass.

Enduring searing pain. Paralyzed as a suffocating darkness closes in. I wake up covered in sweat, alone in my mother's bed. Dena says we'll have to sell the house. Anytime she talks, I wonder what'll happen to me. Until we figure that out, I'll sleep in Mom's sheets so I can still breathe her smell.

I park in the church's lot and take a few moments to collect myself. Eventually I stagger out of my car and my black heels click across the asphalt towards the glass entrance doors. I see Dena talking to the priest and her new boyfriend, Jonathan, is holding her hand. My throat closes as I walk to them. Even in our lowest moment, Dena still has someone to stand beside her. I don't think I've envied my sister more.

"Kim," she says, looking past the priest to me. "Excuse me, Father." She steps away and reaches out, and I collapse into her embrace. Tears pound behind my eyes. I focus on my breath and force the tears away.

"I'm sorry for your loss," Jonathan says and I can tell that he's had practice with this phrase.

I nod stiffly. "Thank you."

We stand there for a few awkward moments before Dena finally says, "It'll be a closed casket, Kimmy."

"Oh." I take a moment to absorb this. "Why?"

Dena winces. "After the accident, they decided this would be a more suitable way to grieve."

"Oh. Okay." I have not seen Mom since the accident and don't really know the full extent of her injuries. They must be bad. My throat constricts. I choke on sobs that come out of nowhere.

"Oh Kimmy," Dena says, pulling me to her again. Her hand runs up and down my back in a smooth rhythm. "It's okay. She's in a better place."

I want to believe this is true, but all I can think about is that "a better place" is away from me. I want to tell my sister so much, to fully disclose the core of my pain. "Dena, I just...with Mom—"

"I think it's best that we talk about that later," Dena interrupts, as if sensing what I'm about to say.

"Oh," I say, slightly taken aback. Why is she denying me this? I try to say something more, but she gives me a pointed look. I drop my eyes and say nothing.

Dena turns away. As I follow her into the church, my heart hardens even more—threatening to break.

Now I'm not just mourning the death of our mother. I'm mourning the loss of my sister, too.

Chapter Twenty-One

TUESDAY, DECEMBER 20, 2005

"What are you doing here?" I ask once Dena has put Summer to bed and returns to the living room. I've poured us each an enormous glass of white zinfandel, knowing that my sister's presence, not to mention her red eyes and singular suitcase, is a clear sign that something's very wrong.

She'd said nothing to me once she'd entered my apartment, only rushed over to Summer to finish her bath, and then given her countless hugs and kisses. I had watched at a safe distance, shifting awkwardly on my heels. I'd grown fond of my private moments with Summer. Dena abruptly showing up and taking over throws me for a lurch. I know it's crazy (she *is* Summer's mother) but it's how I feel.

When Summer first arrived, I thought I'd be desperately awaiting Dena's return. Now I wish we'd had more time. I wasn't a good aunt before—not by half. This was my chance to make up for that. Dena's return puts everything on pause.

My sister accepts the wine and takes a long swallow. Then she sits on the loveseat across from me and scrapes the hair away from her face.

Dena doesn't look good. Her skin is blotchy, her hair's disheveled, and she looks like she hasn't slept in days. She takes a last sip of wine before setting it down on the makeshift coffee table in front of us. "My marriage is falling apart," she says at last.

I watch her steadily, having expected something like this but not being fully prepared for it. "What happened, Dena? You're not due here for four more days."

Her expression strains. She says nothing, but her eyes mist with tears. On instinct, I move to sit next to her, massaging her back as Jillian did for me not that long ago.

"This whole vacation was an attempt to fix our marriage." Her voice is barely a whisper, as if even mentioning their troubles is shameful. "Jonathan and I don't see nearly enough of each other. We're so absorbed in our careers and neither one of us wants to budge an inch. I thought if we spent some quality time together, we could fix things. I felt we needed to try for Summer's sake."

"Of course," I say, knowing the problems many have said began in their broken homes. But I can't help thinking that even through all of their trials, at least those people have parents to whine to.

"We're so different, Kim," she continues, taking in a shuddering breath. "I never saw it before. Maybe it's because we got married so quickly, I don't know. I mean, we don't even like to do the same things."

"What do you mean?"

She takes another gulp of wine and wipes her eyes. "He loves to read. All the time. And watch C-SPAN. It drives me crazy. When I get off work, I like to go out with friends and socialize. He used to do that all the time with me, and then I found out he was just putting up with it for my sake. He'd much rather be a homebody. Given the choice, he'd be stuck in his library for days with Tolstoy and Balzac. I don't understand him. I mean, I'm literary minded, but it's really too much!"

"If you say it is, it must be," I say, rubbing her shoulders. Dena wrote a 250-page thesis for college. I don't think I've read a book that long in my entire life.

"But I'm not like him," she says, shivering from the tears. "He's an English professor. A *gorgeous* English professor," she adds spitefully.

"He is cute," I say, trying to help.

"You're not the only one who thinks so. You should see the girls he teaches. They clamor to be in his class, to be near him. They don't respect that he's married with a child."

"Did he cheat on you?" I ask, sending up a silent prayer that he hasn't.

"No," she says, "but I know he will. Eventually he has to, right? The temptation is too great."

"I don't think that's true. Not if he has a good place to come home to."

"You just don't get it, Kim!" she explodes, then immediately lowers her voice. "He *doesn't* have a good place to come home to. I'm angry all the time. Sometimes I turn into this awful bitch that I don't even recognize. I accuse him of all these horrible things. It's not like me. And I try to stop it, but I can't. And he fights back and slams the door, going off to his library or the university to sulk. I'm so resentful of all the time we spend apart. And of course that makes him want to stay away more." She catches her breath. "We were so close in the beginning. Practically inseparable."

"I remember," I say, and I really do. It was so annoying. "But you two are still good together. I saw it when you were here to drop off Summer."

Dena shakes her head, her tone turning emphatic. "It isn't real. We put on that face for Summer. The minute the door closes, it's like we're different people." She sighs and plunges on. "We probably spend only thirty hours a week together, mostly just sleeping beside each other. The few times at the beginning of our vacation were the only times we've had sex in almost six months."

"Geez, Dena," I say, not really knowing what to say because all this time, I've had a starkly different view of their marriage.

She wipes her dripping eyes. "I don't know what to do now. We had this really awful argument, and I got so angry again. I yelled I wanted a divorce, and he yelled back that he wanted one, too. And I was so shocked to hear him say it because I didn't mean what I said, but he sure looked like he did. So I grabbed my things and took the first flight here and we've not spoken since."

I reach out to embrace her and she weeps on my shoulder. It's so strange, this sudden reversal of roles. Why did I think their marriage was so perfect?

"And I just keep thinking about Summer," Dena whispers. "What's going to happen to her if we get divorced?"

"I don't know," I say, deeply saddened and shaken by all of this. "So, are you going through with it?"

She pulls back and dabs her eyes with the palms of her hands. "Do you have a napkin or something?"

"Sure." I take our glasses to the kitchen sink and return with a log of paper towels.

After blowing her nose several times, Dena looks up at me and says, "I don't know. I told him I wanted a divorce to make him listen to me, to test him. I didn't expect he'd call my bluff. Do you really think he wants a divorce?"

"I don't know."

"He was so angry when he said it, I almost didn't recognize him. Oh, Kim. It was so terrible. We were at this beautiful hotel. We were supposed to be having the time of our lives and instead we spent it bickering and finally—" She stops to blow her nose.

"Maybe he's just angry too. Maybe he just hurled back what you threw at him. He might not want a divorce at all."

"Uh huh," Dena says, hiccupping. "I just—I just don't want it to be over. Or maybe I do, I don't know. I'm so confused. Do you ever get like this, Kim?"

I know the question is rhetorical, but I answer anyway. "Sure I have. I questioned whether I was in love with Jared for the longest time, even though I was sure that I was. Then I realized I just wanted him to love me back so badly that I overlooked the serious flaws in our relationship. When he cheated on me again, I finally had the courage to put up my hands and say no more. I'm still in shock about the breakup, but I'm sure now that I did the right thing."

"But I don't know if I want to divorce Jonathan," Dena says, her eyes threatening more tears.

"Of course, it's not the same for you. You're married with a kid. You don't decide this on a whim. Or on a single argument," I add, hoping the last part is true for her, even though it clearly wasn't for me.

Dena bobs her head and draws a steadying breath. "Thanks."

"You're welcome." Then, after a moment, "Has he tried to call you?"

She shakes her head. "No. And I haven't called him either. We're so stubborn, Kim. Just so damn stubborn!"

"Okay, okay." I stroke her arm. "Let's just forget about it for now. Why don't you get into some pajamas and go sleep with Summer? She's missed you terribly."

"Really?" She glances in her daughter's direction. "I've missed her too. I really have."

"I bet."

Dena's eyes clear as she gazes about my apartment. She sniffs the air. "Your place looks really clean. And it smells good. You've really kept it up."

"Thanks," I say, happy that she's noticed. My apartment hasn't been this clean in almost two years.

"And you have a Christmas tree!" she says, as if seeing it for the first time. "Oh, Kim. Your place looks like a proper home."

My chest warms with pride. It's so rare for Dena to compliment me. "Summer and I picked out the tree and this nice guy helped us set it up. And we bought all sorts of ornaments and lights for it." I grin. "I wanted it to be Summer's home away from home."

"Well, it sure is," Dena says, smiling at me. "You did a really great job with her. All she can talk about is the fun you guys had."

"It was rough at first," I admit. "But it turned good quickly. I actually enjoy having her here. She brings me a sense of..." I pause as I think of the word. "*Peace.*"

Dena's smile is warm and genuine. "You know, I think you'd make a great mother."

"You do?"

"I do. I mean, look how you've transformed this place. Look at you!" Her eyes take me in for once without criticism. "Your skin has never looked better. In fact, you're positively glowing! And you pulled your hair back, which I always thought looked best on you —"

"I know, I know," I say, wondering if there's anyone in the world who actually likes my hair down.

Her eyes light with interest. "Summer mentioned you bought new work clothes," she continues, her tone excited. "Are you getting promoted?"

My happiness fades. "Not exactly. It actually looks like I'll have to quit my job."

"But why?" she says, and I wonder if she even listened to our last phone conversation. Then again, she's had a lot to worry about too.

"Because my co-worker slept with Jared."

"Oh my god! That's right. Sorry."

I sigh wearily. "Anyway, it's just too embarrassing to go back."

Dena nods solemnly. "That's just awful. What an asshole."

"I couldn't agree more."

"So I take it you're using your vacation time?"

"Sick days," I say. "I just don't think I can go back and face her."

"I think that you should," Dena says, her face filling with anger. "I mean, what a bitch to do that to you! I think you should stand toe-to-toe with her and tell her exactly how you feel."

"Maybe," I say, still exhausted from my confrontation with Rachel earlier. "I don't know. Honestly, I don't even want to bother. If I don't see her, I think I can put this whole thing behind me faster."

"Well, you know how I feel," Dena says in her older-sister way. "I'm just saying it would help you."

"We'll see, Dena. But I'm not counting on it."

"Okay." She clears her eyes a final time. As if realizing how much time we've spent talking to each other (a rarity for us), she sits up a little and says, "Well, I guess I'd better get ready for bed. Do you have a shirt that I can wear? In my rush to get out, I think I only packed my toiletries and coat."

"Sure." I disappear into my bedroom. A moment later, I return with the Rice sweatshirt she gave me during her senior year.

When I hand it to her, she grins broadly. "I didn't know you still had this!"

"Sure. I wear it all the time. It's really comfy."

"That's great." She watches as I struggle to move the coffee table in order to accommodate the foldout bed. "Do you need any help?"

I shake my head and scoot the table near the kitchen, then peel off the couch cover that hides hideous, floral print upholstery. The couch pillows are soon a wobbly pile on the floor and I bend to pull the bar.

"Let me help," she insists, now wearing nothing but the sweatshirt that falls just above her knees. "Heave, ho!"

Together, the bed folds out smoothly. I grab the spare comforter and extra pillows from the small linen closet in the hallway and do my best to arrange a comfy bed.

"You sure you're okay sleeping on the couch?" Dena asks. "I can move Summer out here. It's really no problem. I don't want to kick you out of your bedroom, especially when we're the ones imposing on you."

"No, it's fine." I pull off my socks and drape them over the arm of the couch as I scoot beneath the comforter. "Really. Summer slept here a few times without complaining. I'll be fine."

"Thanks again for giving us your bed," Dena says. She turns to go, but pauses.

"You okay?" I ask, watching her.

She nods, but returns to the foldout bed and sits carefully at the edge, just beside my feet. "Kim?"

"What?"

"I wanted to say I'm sorry about how I talked to you on the phone the other night."

I blink at her. "What do you mean?"

"When you talked about Mom. I snapped at you. I shouldn't have done that."

"That's okay," I say, having gotten over the conversation since Summer confided that Mom's death still affects my sister.

"No," Dena says firmly, "it's not. You're my baby sister and if you want to talk about Mom, I shouldn't shut you up. It's just..." Her voice trails and her eyes brim with tears. "I was having such a rough time with Jonathan that talking about Mom brought back all these old feelings that I didn't need."

"It's okay, Dena. Really. It's okay."

"I think about her a lot," she says. "About the accident."

My throat tightens. I fight to keep my voice steady. "What about it?"

"You know," she says, blinking hard. "Just—if she meant to crash into that tree. If it really was an accident or on purpose."

"The roads were slick," I tell her, flashing to when I was younger, defending our mother with these same words. "It'd just rained. Why would she do it on purpose?"

"You didn't know," Dena says, her voice thick with grief. "Mom was depressed. *Really* depressed. She'd been that way for a long time. She was taking all these medications and had been off them a few weeks before the accident."

The world shifts under me. None of it felt real. "But she wouldn't leave us. She wouldn't. She loved us."

Dena reaches to touch my hand. "I know she loved us. But, Kim, sometimes severe depression affects people in ways that seem out-of-character."

She still doesn't think it was an accident. And after all this time...

My eyes burn. *If it wasn't an accident, then—*

But the thought is too terrible, and I shake my head in rising anger. How could she? I had no place to go, no extended family. When Dena left home, she left me too—alone.

"I'm not saying I know anything for sure," Dena amends upon seeing my face. "I'm just laying out the facts as they were told to me. With Dad's death and her losing her job..."

"She didn't lose her job!" I snap, my voice unintentionally strong. But it's because I know Dena is wrong, and if she's wrong in this, maybe she's wrong about everything else. "She was gone every morning before I took the bus, like always. She *didn't* lose her job."

"She did," Dena says quietly. "She called me at school. She said she was desperate for money and didn't know what to do. I gave her as much as I could from some cash scholarships to tie her over, but it wasn't much."

Good grief. I knew we were poor, but I never realized it had been so bad that Mom needed to borrow money from my sister.

"Her part-time job carried the mortgage," Dena continues. "When she lost it, she didn't know how she was going to make ends meet. And she was exhausted all the time..."

"I remember," I say as a memory surfaces. I'd returned from school to find Mom asleep in the same position I'd seen her in bed that morning. So I'd shaken her, worried that she was sick. "It's okay, Kimmy," my mother said groggily as she slowly woke up.

"Are you okay?"

"I'm fine. I'm fine." She closed her eyes. "I'm just tired. Let me sleep some more, okay? Wait another hour and then come and wake me..."

I stare at my sister with a heavy heart. "I don't know what to say, other than I still believe it was an accident."

Dena's eyebrows raise. "You do?"

"Yes," I say, needing to believe it more than anything else. I loved our mother. I have to believe that she would never intentionally leave us alone in this world. "Yes, I do."

"I want to believe that too," she says, looking impossibly sad. "But I just can't. All these suspicions keep coming back. All these questions. I wish I could just wake up tomorrow morning and believe what you do." She sighs and lowers her eyes. "It would be so much easier to believe that."

"You can, Dena. We loved Mom. Even if she was depressed, even if she lost her job, she would never willingly do something that would hurt us. We were the Three Musketeers, remember?" My throat closes and I choke on a sob.

"I remember," she says. "I want to believe that."

I reach out to hug her and we cry together. All the years and distance between us surfaces with dizzying force. We were both devastated by our mother's death and had handled it in different ways. Years may have passed, but we are still recovering.

"I want to be a better sister to you," Dena says, wiping her eyes. "I'm so sorry for the way I've treated you. I was just so angry at Mom. I wanted us to have a better life, but she couldn't keep it together. All the time I kept wishing we'd had more, and that we weren't always struggling. And I was awful to you—"

"Dena, it's okay," I say, my anger dissipating. "Really. You were so young when she died. We both were. I wish we could have been closer during that time..."

"I'm so sorry for that!" she cries and her shoulders quake. "I was so stupid! So selfish and stupid."

"Shhh, it's okay." I pull her tight, holding her like she used to hold me. "Really, Dena. I've forgiven you. It'll be okay."

"I feel so lost," she whispers. "So alone. I wish Mom were here."

"Me too." I hold her tight and kiss her hair, wishing I could squeeze out all our hurt and loneliness, put us back to when Mom was alive. Change things.

I wonder how differently we would have turned out if Mom hadn't died. Would Dena have moved so far away? Would I have pursued college and had an actual career? Would I be married, having not dated jerks out of loneliness and despair? Would I now have a kid or two of my own? Would I even be the same person, or would I be a better one?

Dena lets out a long sigh and pulls away. Her smile is tremulous, and her eyes glow warmly in the lamplight. "I do love you, Kim. I'm so sorry for everything I've done to hurt you."

"Me too," I say, feeling closer to her than ever before.

She stands from the couch and looks down at me. There is a fondness in her eyes that is still so foreign. "Do you want to sleep with Summer and me?"

"No." I shake my head. "I'll be fine out here. My bed really isn't meant for three people."

She laughs before catching herself. "I'm sorry about you and Jared. You deserve better, Kim. You really do."

"Thanks." I pull the comforter up to my chin. "And I think you and Jonathan will work out."

"You do?" she asks hopefully.

"I do. You love each other, and that counts for an awful lot."

She nods and paces toward the bedroom. "See you in the morning."

"Goodnight."

Once I hear the door close, I shut off the light and lie still in the darkness. I think about Mom and try to remember clues of her depression. I remember her being so tired and achy after coming home from work. I remember her sleeping too much, not wanting to move, telling me to wake her later, *always* later. But mostly I remember the good times, like singing Beatles melodies with her on the drive to school, or the day she spent all that money to buy me the perfect prom dress.

"I miss you, Mami," I say, wondering if she can hear me.

My cell phone blinks silently next to me. Jared's number flashes across the screen and for a moment I almost answer it.

But in the distance, in memory, I hear my mother say, "Let it go, honey. Let it go."

I turn off my phone and hold the image of my mother's face close to my heart as I slowly drift off to sleep.

Chapter Twenty-Two

The next morning I wake up early and sneak into my bedroom, careful not to wake Dena and Summer, who sleep cuddled together on my bed. I ease a pair of exercise shorts and a sports bra out of my bureau and return to the living room, where I quickly change and return the foldout bed to the couch and the linens to the closet.

I turn on the television and put the volume near mute as I root around for my mother's old Susan Powter exercise tape, something we used to work out to in the 90s. After some effort, I find it and slide the cassette into the VCR (a technology going by the wayside, I know, but I'm wary to give it up since I'd have to buy so many replacement DVDs). My next task is to remove the old step box from beneath the loveseat. It's so dusty that I have to wipe it clean with a wet paper towel before setting it up on the floor.

As I start my workout, I reflect that this is the first time I've begun an exercise routine before January 2nd. It's always been a New Year's resolution, but one I never fully commit to past the initial weeks of the year. I walk in place and then step side to side, lifting my arms as the instructor dictates, then—as quietly as possible—

placing my right foot on the box, stepping off, and then alternating feet. I have to modify fairly quickly, but at least I'm off my butt and actually moving.

The last time I seriously exercised was many years ago when I briefly joined Dena in running, and even then I only managed one lousy 5k while she was off doing half marathons. Since then, the most I've done to increase my heart rate is to climb the stairs to work every morning. In ten minutes, sweat fuses my sports bra to my chest. I'm relieved there aren't any witnesses, because my stomach fat is jiggling more than ever, not to mention my untoned arms and legs.

After the thirty-minute workout, which I'm barely able to finish, I turn off the TV, rearrange the step box beneath the loveseat, and spread out a towel on the floor so that I can do some crunches. Grunting from the effort, I only manage ten before I'm ready to pass out. *Good enough for today,* I think. *Better not overdo it.*

I slip into the bathroom for a quick shower and emerge in a robe with a white towel twirled like a turban above my head.

"I thought I heard you working out this morning," Dena says, coming from the kitchen with two steaming mugs of coffee.

"Sorry, did I wake you?" I take the mug from her and sip carefully. Dena's always known how to make the perfect cup: two scoops of sugar with a splash of cream.

"No, I was already up." She sits at the kitchen table and draws one knee into her chest. "I couldn't really sleep."

I sit across from her. "Has Jonathan called?"

She shakes her head and sets down the mug. She looks so vulnerable with her coffee and oversized sweatshirt.

I reach out to touch her hand. "It'll be okay, Dena. You'll work this out."

"Yeah. We'll see." She retracts her hand and lifts the mug to her lips. "So, what's your plan for the day?"

I adjust the towel on my head as I sit back. "Actually, I was planning to go Christmas shopping for you and Summer." I grin and add, "Sorry, you're not invited."

"Oh, Kim. You don't have to get us anything."

"I still am. And you better like it."

She nods and smiles slightly. "Okay, then. We'll probably just stay here or maybe go see a matinee. We've a lot of catching up to do."

"So, where is the munchkin?" I ask, looking about.

"Still asleep."

"Really? Normally she's up—"

"—really early," Dena finishes and we chuckle knowingly together. "But she didn't move an inch when I got up, so I figured I'd let her sleep in."

"That's probably a good idea," I say, taking another sip. "Good coffee, Dena."

"Thanks." She smiles and we sit in silence for a while.

"I think I may go into work tomorrow," I say at length.

"Really?"

"Well, only long enough to turn in my resignation. I just can't work in the same office as Lisa. It'd be just awful, and they don't pay me nearly enough for that."

Dena takes another sip, considering. "But what will you do for work?"

I unwrap the towel from my head and drape it over my knees. My mousy hair hangs in damp tendrils about my face and I scrape it back with my fingers. "All I can do is get another job and live off my savings until then. It's probably for the best, anyway. I've always hated this job. And I think it's time for a change." I almost tell her I'm thinking about going to college, but quickly stop myself. Knowing Dena, if it doesn't work out, she'll harp on me about it forever. She made it through college, medical school, and beyond and I'm certain she secretly wonders why I haven't mustered up the courage to just do it. While I know last night was a wonderful bridge for our broken relationship, it's still hard for me to fully open up to her.

"Good for you," Dena says and raises her mug. "A toast to you and your new start!"

I roll my eyes but obligingly clink my mug with hers, grateful that she supports my decision to quit. Then I drain my coffee, stand up, and put my mug in the sink. "I'm going to get dressed," I announce. "You need anything?"

"Nothing at all," Dena says, holding her mug in both hands as she polishes off the steaming remnants.

"Okay." I lean down to give her a quick kiss on the cheek before I disappear.

On my way down to the car, I nearly collide with Alice, who's coming up the stairs balancing three empty boxes. I ask if she needs any help.

"I'm fine!" she says cheerily. Then, after giving my wool skirt, heels, and silk blouse (visible at the V of my buttoned pea coat) a thorough glance, she adds, "And you look too nice for this sort of work, anyway."

"Please," I insist, easing a box from her grip. "What can I do to help?"

"You sure?"

"Positive."

"Okay," she says with obvious relief. "If you wouldn't mind helping me with a few of these..." And I follow her into her old apartment that now looks like a warehouse. Alice has stacked boxes in every available space, shredded packing tape across the carpet, and assorted Sharpies and neon index cards on her breakfast table.

She hands me another small box then, asking if it's too heavy, slides one more on top. Alice balances her load with her chin as we shuffle down the stairs and across the parking lot, stopping at her green SUV.

"Thanks." She pushes our load on top of the boxes already arranged in the backseat. "Brandon should be here any minute to help, but I prefer getting the small stuff out of the way first, since it takes the longest."

"Sure," I say, handing her the last box.

"So, how is your boyfriend? Jared, wasn't it?"

"Yeah," I say, looking away. "We're not together."

"What do you mean? Did you two break up?"

"A while ago."

"Really?"

"Yeah. He cheated on me." I immediately regret saying this last part and flush the bright shade of a lobster.

Alice reaches out and embraces me. I flinch, but she doesn't let go. Gradually I fall into the embrace, pleasant and languid as sunwarmed honey. "I'm so sorry," she murmurs into my hair. "I know how much that hurts."

"Thanks." I pull back, trying to hide my budding emotions. "It's okay, though. I'm adjusting."

Alice's lips curve into a coy smile.

"What?" I ask, instantly suspicious.

"Nothing. It's silly." She shuts the door to her car and adjusts the scarf about her neck as we start back up the stairs.

"What? You can tell me."

She chuckles. "It's just that my brother mentioned you."

I hadn't expected this and don't know quite how to respond. "Oh?"

We reach her flat and organize a few more boxes to carry down to the car. "I told him once that if you were single, you'd be just his type."

I make my way back down the stairs, careful not to drop anything. "Why is that?"

"Isn't it obvious? You're smart, funny, pretty, and very sweet. Just his type."

"That's kind of you," I say, passing over my two boxes. "But I'm not ready to get back out there just yet."

"No, of course not," she says. She finishes up and closes the SUV.

"He is very nice, though," I add as an afterthought.

"It's okay to take your time, Kim," Alice says. "Lord knows you deserve it."

The mall isn't nearly as congested as it was a few days ago. *Probably because everyone already finished Christmas shopping,* I think with a wry smile. First stop is the toy store where I saw the most adorable stuffed unicorn when I came in with Summer a few days ago. Naturally, this is the most crowded store in the mall, but I take a few controlled breaths and try not to let the claustrophobia kick in.

"This is the new me," I say to myself, making this my mantra. I squeeze past the action figure section and maneuver to the stuffed animal aisle. To my surprise, there are dozens of unicorns of various sizes, shapes, and colors. There is even one that's bigger than I am. Out of curiosity, I pull back the price tag at its ear and gasp, "Three hundred dollars!"

"You should see the ones at FAO Schwarz," says a woman as she squeezes past me. "They cost as much as my first car."

I gaze up at the rows of unicorns in despair. How can I possibly decide? Summer would like them all!

It's at that moment that I see a saleswoman arranging a medium-sized, ivory-colored unicorn near the bottom row. Something clicks inside me. On instinct, I rush over before any of the other parents snatch it up. The stuffed animal is impossibly soft. When I press it against my chest, it actually feels like the unicorn's hugging me back. Around its neck is a satiny red and white Christmas bow with gold edging.

It's perfect.

I walk up to the cashier and leave the store with my first Christmas present swinging in a bag beside my hip. The pride reaches my fingertips. This gift will be something that Summer can always remember me by.

Next up is Jillian. I've already given some thought to her present and scour the beauty department for the perfect perfume, finally settling on a light, coconut-infused scent with a matching body lotion. I also find a set of earrings that I know Dena will enjoy (small sterling silver hoops with three gliding crystal beads) and a red cashmere blend sweater.

The one who takes the longest is Jonathan. In a moment of sheer optimism that my brother-in-law will still be with my sister after the holidays, I enter a bookstore and glance through twelve aisles stuffed with every type of book I can imagine. Since I don't read for pleasure, I don't know any author that Jonathan might like, much less what he's already read. Thirty minutes pass and I'm no nearer to a selection than when I arrived.

I'm just passing the magazine rack when I notice the newest edition of *Working Mother*. On its cover is an attractive, thirty-something woman in a fitted suit, smiling brightly with the confidence of someone who has her life completely under control.

"Maybe that can be me," I think, reflecting that the last time I saw such a magazine was with Summer in a supermarket, struggling to rein her tantrum. How things have changed since then.

I'm just about to leave when I catch sight of a leather-bound, gold-leafed edition of *War and Peace*. The thick volume is an iron weight between my hands. I turn to the first page, loving its musky, smoky scent and how Old English script marks the chapter titles.

Jonathan probably already has it, but maybe he'd appreciate its beauty. I turn it over in my hands as if it's a precious, unearthed jewel. I remember Dena saying how he'd rather spend his days locked away reading Tolstoy or Balzac. Since I don't know who the latter writer is, I'd say *War and Peace* is thematically appropriate for what's been happening to our family.

I also pick up a copy of *Working Mother* on my way to the cashier, thrilled with my new purchases that swing heavily by my side. I've never bought Christmas gifts for so many people in my life. For the last few years, it's just been for Jillian and Jared, with a combined gift shipped to Dena, Summer, and Jonathan, and almost always late. Well, not this year. I'm changing. And everyone can get a present as a fortunate result.

Just as I'm making my way through the food court, my mobile rings and I switch the bags to my left hand in order to see who it is. An unfamiliar number flashes across the screen and I instinctively answer it. "Hello?"

"Is this Kimberly Kincaid?" says a voice, which I unsuccessfully try to place.

"This is she." I revert to my office tone. "May I ask who's calling?"

"Ms. Kincaid, this is Heather from the health clinic. I have some news."

Great. Nurse Arthritis wants me back for further testing. "What news?" I ask as I squeeze past a line of people waiting for yogurt smoothies.

"Why don't you stop by the clinic later today and we can discuss—"

"Oh, please don't make me go back there," I say in a rush. "Just tell me what it is. Do I need more tests? Is it HPV or something?"

"Nothing like that. Actually, I'd say congratulations are in order." She laughs nervously. "You're pregnant."

I stop dead in my tracks, and a man instantly collides into my back.

"Watch it, lady!" he snaps, pushing past.

"Mrs. Kincaid?" Nurse Heather says. "Are you—"

"Pregnant?" I stammer, wondering if I'd had a stroke. "How can I be pregnant? I've—how...?"

"The urine test for your physical confirmed it," she says in a very business-like manner. "Actually, we had the results when you were here before, but they got mixed up with someone else's and we only just now confirmed it. We wanted to contact you to ensure that you set up an appointment with your gynecologist for some further testing. You *are* on a multi-vitamin, correct? Something with a folic acid additive?"

"No," I say weakly.

"That's the first thing you should do then," she continues. "Folic acid is very important for a growing fetus."

"How pregnant am I?"

There's a pause. "Well, *very* pregnant."

I quickly rephrase, "I mean, how far along?"

"It's pretty early, by our estimates." There's a pause, followed by the sound of flipping paper. "You noted your last heavy period was in mid-October and it's almost the New Year. So just a little over two months. But of course, you'll need an ultrasound to confirm an actual due date..."

Oh my god. I thought I had a period a month ago, but was that really just spotting? *Oh my god! Oh my god! Oh my god!*

"Now, if you'd like, we can put you in touch with several reputable gynecologists. I figured since it's been several years since your last Pap smear that you may not have a regular doctor."

"No, I don't..." I hardly know what to say, much less feel. "I have to go."

"If you have further questions, please don't hesitate—"

I end the call and stand there in the middle of the mall, clutching my bags stupidly in my arms. Pregnant? *Pregnant?*

I rack my brain for the last time I had sex. And then—*Oh my god!* This means Jared will have to come back into my life. What will he say when he finds out? Should he find out? Do I even *want* a baby?

I slump onto a bench and pile the bags beside me. A group of parents stride past, doing their best to keep their children in order.

How can I possibly raise a child? I have no job. No husband. And no solid prospects for either. How can this possibly work?

Itching for a drag, I root through my purse for a full minute before remembering Jillian's crusade against my smoking. The flushing of all of my cigarettes, even my emergency stashes, down the toilet.

I guess it's just as well. You can't smoke or drink when you're pregnant.

Then I think about the drinks that I've had, and that time I was drunk, and all of those cigarettes I couldn't resist,

Oh my god. What if I've already harmed the baby?

My head itches. The first beads of sweat trickle down my temples. I reach into my purse and remove my compact, but as I open the case to reapply my powder, I'm shocked by my reflection. I don't recognize myself at all.

I snap the compact closed. *No.* If I'm pregnant, then I'm pregnant. What's done is done. I'll just have to find some way to make this work.

I sit with that for a long time. Maybe this baby's meant to be. I've been alone for so long. Maybe this is a cosmic gift. My karma, *good* karma, catching up with me.

But as I make my way back to the car, a sudden chill pumps through my veins. What about Jared? Do I tell him? Not tell him? What will I do once Dena and Summer leave?

I see myself stranded with an infant, living in an apartment I can't afford. Without a job and without help.

How can this possibly work?

Chapter Twenty-Three

SUNDAY, NOVEMBER 21, 1999

I hold my sister's hand loosely, not quite expecting it to move, yet painfully hoping it will. It is a small hand, cool to the touch, with long fingernails painted burgundy red. I remember Mom saying we can learn a lot about people by their hands.

The IV drip fluids into its little plastic bag and the elevators outside the ICU ding open. It's been two hours since they cut my niece from my sister's body. From what I understand, Dena suffered a placental abruption and the resulting blood loss nearly killed her and the baby. Several transfusions and many strained looks from the medical staff later, she now rests with the aid of what looks like a heavy dose of Xanax.

I open an *Entertainment Weekly* across my lap and read while still holding Dena's hand. I massage her cool skin, hoping to give her warmth.

It's a long time before Dena moves and when she does, it nearly startles me off the chair. "Dena?" I say, dropping the magazine and gazing at my sister over the bed-rail. "Hey, are you awake?"

She stirs and then settles with a sigh beneath the sheets. I take in her slight form, the ashen skin, the tubes and things protruding all over her body, the enormous blue oxygen mask that threatens to eat the whole of her lower face. "Dena?" I say again, worried now. "Come on, honey. Wake up and talk to me."

She moves and her head of dark wet curls splays starkly across the bleach-white sheets. Her eyes slowly open, close, then open again and she peers at me as if through fog.

When she mumbles something, I snatch up her hand. "I'm here, Dena. I'm here. Your little sister's here."

Her dark eyes dart about the room before finally meeting mine. In that moment, we lock in both mind and spirit. The past years that have divided us momentarily fade away. For once, we are equals. Perhaps never again.

"The baby?" Dena mummers, her breath fogging the mask.

"The baby's fine, Dena. Just fine. You made it." I will back the hot tears as I put her hand to my mouth and kiss her fingers. *She's going to be okay,* I think. *My sister's going to be okay!*

Dena visibly relaxes and slowly closes her eyes. I keep her fingers pressed gently to my lips, grateful for the warmth of my sister's skin.

I smile down at her and—as if on inspiration—lean over. I brush my lips across Dena's temple and slowly back away, taking up my vigil by her hospital bed, my sister's hand small and still in my lap.

The ICU door opens and Jonathan strides inside. "How is she?" he asks, his face pale and tight with worry.

"She's fine," I say, standing to offer my chair. "She's sleeping now."

"Did she say anything?" He grasps for her hand as he sits beside her.

"Only to ask about the baby."

"I haven't seen her," he says, staring down hard at his wife. "Have you?"

"The baby?" I shake my head. "Not really. The doctors took her away when they started working on Dena." I remember the baby's glistening, bloodied form being lifted from Dena's distended belly and how it had cried out in the corner of the OR, to everyone's relief.

"Oh," he says. There are a few strained moments before his tear-stained eyes meet mine. "Will you check on her? Make sure she's okay?"

"Sammrr," Dena murmurs against the oxygen mask.

Jonathan starts. "Dena? Honey?"

She shifts a little in the bed. "Sammrr," she says again, unintelligibly.

Jonathan moves the oxygen mask partly aside. "What are you trying to say, baby? Are you in pain?"

"Her name," she croaks. "I want her name to be Summer."

She says this and I glance outside the window, at the snow that fills the pane like finely shaved ice. *Summer? She's naming her kid after the warmest season of the year in the middle of winter?* I glance down at Dena and think that the drugs she's on must be pretty fine.

"Summer," says Jonathan. "Of course. Whatever you want." He picks up Dena's hand and kisses it. "Whatever you want."

Dena sighs and groggily picks up her other hand. It hovers momentarily in the air before Jonathan catches it. Then she falls asleep.

"Will you...?" he asks me at length.

"Of course." I walk outside and down the bleached hallway. A nurse directs me to the neonatal unit. After some minutes, I am brought to an enormous, white plastic incubator with a heavy blanket thrown over the top to prevent the intrusion of too much light. A small, pink, two-month early wrinkled baby sleeps inside, with little tubes—like her mother—protruding from her arms and mouth.

"Hello, Summer," I say, pressing my hand against the warm plastic, the same hand that had held her mother's just minutes earlier. My heart fills with a strange warmth, and I know what it is: love. It is instantaneous, unconditional, and forever. I yearn to have a baby like this someday: someone to love and who loves me back.

I smile as my eyes fill with tears and whisper, "Welcome to the world, little girl."

Chapter Twenty-Four

I'm going back to work to face Lisa. I'm still pregnant—going on eighteen hours of not telling a soul. And I'm still scared, but at least the shock has worn off and I can now say that nothing else can surprise me—unless Lisa herself is pregnant by Jared too and then our children will be half-siblings. But then the world would be far too cruel and—as you can see—it wouldn't be a surprise, as I've already guessed.

I slip on my favorite new ensemble: the fitted black suit with the ivory camisole. Then, after following Jillian's makeup advice down to the last brush stroke, I square myself in my new close-toed black heels. All of which might have been a tad overdressed for a secretary, but I don't care. I'm the new-and-improved Kim Kincaid.

Now I'm standing at the crosswalk two blocks from the office. Just as the WALK sign illuminates, a hand touches my elbow.

"Excuse me?" says a young woman with dark auburn hair and a ready smile.

"Yes?" I say in surprise.

"Do you know where—" She consults a crinkled slip of paper. "—the administration building is? Room 407?"

"That's actually where I work," I say, pointing the way. "I can show you."

"Thanks so much!"

We walk together and suddenly I'm curious. I would have never asked before, but my suit must be empowering me because I ask, "So what do you do here? Do you teach or something?"

She laughs and shakes her head. "Not yet. No, I'm a student."

"Really?" This surprises me. "What's your major?"

"English lit. I went back to school almost three years ago and next semester will be my last before I can finally graduate."

"That's amazing. Wow! You did it in three years?"

"With lots of summer school," she admits. "There were really no breaks. But it wasn't a choice for me. I pull full waiting shifts on weekends and have to take out loans to make ends meet, so the sooner I finish, the better." She smiles and shakes her head again. "But it'll be worth it in the end."

"Really?"

"Really. I couldn't have survived otherwise. I was making less than ten dollars an hour. Now I might finally break forty thousand."

"As what?"

"A teacher. It's something I've always wanted to do ever since I was a kid. My parents are high school teachers, so I guess it's in the blood." She smiles and extends her hand as we walk. "My name's Frieda, by the way."

"Kim," I say, shaking her hand. "So what made you decide to go back? Just the paycheck?"

Her grin broadens. "Admittedly, that was an enormous factor. On my current salary, I could never afford to buy a decent car, much less health insurance or even a house. But really it's because my dream has always been to teach. So one day I decided to just do it."

I open the door to the administration building and we climb the stairs together. I unbutton my coat and hang it over my elbow. It swings in time with my strides. "That's amazing what you're doing. It takes a lot to go back to school."

"Are you a professor here?"

"Professor?" I laugh in shock. "No, no. I'm a secretary."

"Oh." Frieda takes in my pristine suit. "Did you graduate from here?"

"Well, no," I say, thinking about my overly accomplished sister. We're opposites in so many ways and yet—amazingly—are still family. "But I am thinking about it."

"I completely recommend it," she says as we reach the third floor. "It's totally changed my life. My daughter is so proud of me for doing this."

"You have a daughter *too*?" I'm in awe that she can somehow go to school, work, and support a child without exploding.

Frieda chuckles. "All I can say is thank goodness she's a teenager! I know very few parents say that, but it's true for me. I don't think I could handle doing all of this if she were still a baby."

Looks like I'll have to, I think with a grimace. "Well, it was nice meeting you. Good luck with everything."

"Thanks." She waves at me. "And good luck if you decide to come here."

I'm within three steps of the office door. My heart pounds so hard I think others will surely be able to see it through my blouse. I seize the doorknob, turn it, and step inside.

Lisa glances up from her computer. Her face pales as she lurches upwards. "Hi, Kim. You look—different."

I fold my arms across my chest and meet her gaze. Lisa's appearance now looks overly accessorized. Her outfit threadbare. Her six-inch heels completely inappropriate. Had I never really seen Lisa before? "Well. You look just the same to me."

"I'm actually going on break." She doesn't meet my eyes as she pushes past me and swings the door shut behind her.

What a coward. I pull the scarf from my neck and hang up my coat. *Okay then.* I take a breath. *Just today. I can make it through one last day.* I haven't really decided how to tell my bosses I'm quitting, so I'm giving myself the next few hours to figure out my approach.

I log onto my computer and surf the various tabloid websites when Larry strides out of his office. "Hello, Kim," he says, his voice unnaturally pleasant.

"Hi." I instantly minimize the window on my computer. Then click again. Oh my god. *People's* website has frozen across my desktop.

I quickly scoot my chair in front of my screen and smile up at him, realizing I shouldn't be so nervous considering I am about to quit.

"Feel better?" he asks, standing before me.

"Yep," I say, remembering in time that I had called in sick. "Lots. Thanks for asking."

"Sure. You look very nice today."

"Thank you." He's never said that to me before.

"So..." He glances about the office. "Is Lisa on break?"

"She just stepped out."

"I see. Well..." His voice trails and he shrugs. "Anyway, this is from Paul and me. Merry Christmas." He hands me a box of Godiva chocolates wrapped in shiny gold paper.

"Wow. Thank you." I've gotten them nothing. How awkward it will be to quit now that I've received a present from them. "Um, Merry Christmas to you too."

"Any plans for the holiday?"

"Nope." I want him to leave so badly that I can't stand it. "Just spending it with family."

"That's nice." He rocks back on his heels. "We're planning to drive down to Texas to visit the in-laws. You know, load the clan in the mini-van and brave the traffic."

I'm wondering if he actually has anything work-related for me to do. "Sounds nice."

"So let me ask you a question, Kim."

"Yes?" *Did he notice my frozen desktop?*

"Of all the places to get fast-food hamburgers, where do you like to go?"

"Hamburgers?" I echo dumbly. "Like Burger King?"

"I guess if you want to include corporate chains," he says, chuckling humorlessly. "What's your favorite?"

No one's ever asked me this, so it takes a few seconds to answer. "I guess Wendy's."

"And why's that?" he asks, clearly disappointed.

"I like their square-shaped patties. How they're bigger than the bun itself."

"I see. Personally, I like Mr. Burger and Red Robin. They add spices that are more unique than the others. I can't quite tell what they are. Maybe red pepper flakes? Anyway, I find they're far superior."

"That's nice," I say, wondering how the hell I got engaged in this verbal nightmare. I'm reminded of the time I was reviewing a stack of court transcripts and came across a hilarious—at least to me—criticism of my boss, who'd slipped into one of his usual tangential speeches. "Please, Mr. Thomson," said the cantankerous judge. "Just get to the point before I die of old age."

"So would you consider trying any of those two choices?" he asks me.

"Um, sure," I say, even though I've already forgotten the two choices.

"Red Robin or Mr. Burger. I think you'll notice a difference. Their spices, Kim, are far superior. I believe..."

As he rambles on and on, I think back to my first day of work. I was taking notes for Larry in his office and he'd gone off about the best way to get to our office building from the interstate. By minute ten, I turned drowsy. I think I was asleep for about three seconds before I jerked wildly awake. Larry had been staring at his papers and didn't even notice.

Having never fallen asleep while someone was talking to me, I'd adapted to Larry's speeches. Since his lectures circle on themselves like a broken record, I've formed the habit of picking out key nouns and verbs to get the gist without really listening—and thus risk falling asleep again.

In the meantime, I think about the baby that's growing steadily inside me as I "listen" to my boss lecture me about—what?

"—I figure it's probably some hot pepper, perhaps a chili pepper or bell pepper..."

Peppers. Ugh. I will not miss this job.

I covertly glance at the door, wondering when Lisa will return. She must feel as unsettled in this office as I do now. It's her fault, though. The hateful bitch. I hope she stays with Jared so he can cheat on her, too. It'd be the perfect revenge.

What to do about this baby, though? My right hand comes to rest on the slight bulge in my middle that I'd thought was accumulating fat. What will Dena say when she finds out? And Jillian? How am I going to handle this?

Six months ago, I'd have ended this pregnancy without hesitation. Other than a very weak moment when Dena was in the hospital, I've never really wanted children—especially not without a husband. But caring for Summer has opened my eyes to possibility, a life of something more than myself. Something has shifted inside that I can't explain. I've changed—am changing—but I'm still scared and wonder how I'm going to make it on my own with a child.

I sense that Larry's speech is drawing to a close. "Anyway," he says, "I hope you try some new fast-food joints. I'm sure you'll be impressed."

"I will. And thanks for the chocolates. You really shouldn't have."

"It's no problem." He positions a matching box of chocolates in Lisa's chair before returning to his office.

Once his door clicks closed, I heave a sigh and reboot my computer, spending the next few hours surfing the web and returning e-mails guiltlessly. Just as it's nearing my lunch hour, the office door opens and Lisa shuffles to her desk, silently picking up her chocolates and setting them beside her keyboard.

She won't even look at me. I guess she didn't expect to see my face again. "Hello, Lisa," I call over to her.

She says nothing. Instead, she wiggles her mouse and surfs the Internet.

"Still fucking Jared?" I ask, surprised at my candor.

Lisa looks over at me, her eyes wide. "*Excuse* me?"

"I asked if you're still fucking Jared." I cross my arms as renewed strength fills my veins.

Her face etches with guilt. Can it be the Devil is sorry for what she's done? Or perhaps she's just upset that I'm disturbing her perfect universe.

"I knew he was cheating with you," I hear myself saying. "But I blocked it out, hoping it couldn't be true. Tell me, Lisa. What in the hell were you thinking going after someone else's boyfriend? Especially someone you work with?"

She looks struck dumb. Then she seems to gather her resources enough to scowl and say, "I always knew you were a bitch."

"Really?" I have much better names for her. "What did I ever do to you?"

"Nothing!" she spits out. "And everything. You with your to-hell attitude and your perfect boyfriend—"

Perfect? Ha! She really is setting herself up for disappointment if she thinks Jared is perfect.

"I never liked you," she says. "Turns out, neither does Jared."

This last part falls hollow because, of course, I know Jared likes me—or did. He even loved me in his own selfish way. Lisa is firing blanks, and it tears her apart that I know this.

"I see," I say as I stand. Ironically, Lisa has just given me the strength to do what needs to be done.

"What are you doing?" Her eyes narrow in suspicion.

"Shut up." She flinches as I pass her desk, which makes me smile. In four steps, I'm to my boss's door, knocking firmly. After a muffled affirmative, I stride inside, shut the door, and take a seat in front of his desk. "Hello, Larry."

"Yes?" He looks up from his papers. "Are there any messages?"

I straighten. "Just one. I won't be returning after the first of this year. Sorry to quit on such short notice."

His mouth hangs open. "Quit? You're quitting? But—why? Is something not working out for you here?"

"Funny you should say that." I smile sweetly as I smooth back my hair that's fastened into a professional French twist. "It *is* my working conditions. They have become quite..." I let my voice trail dramatically as I pretend to search for the right word. "Unbearable."

"Unbearable?" he asks, flummoxed. "Do you mind if I ask why?"

I meet his gaze with a touch of sadness that isn't all that hard to muster. "It's Lisa."

"Lisa?" His genuine surprise makes me think he was always blind to our office relationship.

"Yes. Unfortunately, last week I discovered that she's been sleeping with my boyfriend. Well, ex-boyfriend now." Larry's eyes grow very wide. I don't care if I've smeared Lisa's reputation. She deserves every ounce of return-play. "That's actually why I called in sick. I'm sure you can understand why I couldn't face her immediately afterward."

"No, no," he stammers. "I suppose not."

"I'm sorry, Larry," I say, meaning it. Preferably, I'd not quit so abruptly, but I'm elated to start my new life. "I'll arrange everything with human resources. I'll use the rest of of my vacation days to cover the rest of today and the few days during the holiday."

"Okay," he says and stops. "*Today*? You're leaving today?"

"Yes. I just had another confrontation with Lisa, so I'm sure you'll understand why I'm choosing to leave immediately." I pointedly glance at my watch. "Actually, in about three minutes."

"Three minutes?"

"Yes."

"I see." He slowly nods. "I understand."

"Thank you, Larry. For everything." I stand and reach across the table and shake his hand diplomatically.

"You too, Kim." He stands up, looking at me. "And there's nothing we can do to change your mind?"

"No, sir," I say. "I'm sorry. It would be too hard to face Lisa each morning."

But of course it's not just Lisa. Her betrayal has been the much-needed catalyst to uproot me from my dead-end job. I was going nowhere in this stagnant state, so it was just as well that I get out of here now rather than let another few years—or decades—pass me by.

"Thank you for coming in today," Larry says. "Do you want me to tell Paul?"

"I'll tell him myself," I say with a smile. "Thanks for under-standing."

"What are you doing?" Lisa hisses as I shut Larry's door.

I ignore her and enter Paul's office. I tell him exactly what I told Larry and both are very sorry that I'm leaving, but are perfectly understanding about it. Of course, I secretly wanted them to offer firing Lisa as an incentive to stay, but am not really surprised when they don't. After all, she's the least expendable of the two of us, although I'm comforted that their trust in her has eroded. I know now that she'll never leave this job, and at least I have a chance for something better.

It doesn't take long to pack up my desk. Actually, it doesn't even take thirty seconds. I never really made it a home here, with pictures of family or adorable paperweights. The most personal thing at my desk is a purple fuzzy pen that Jillian got me for Valentine's Day. Everything else belongs to the office.

When Dena calls announcing she and Summer are in the parking lot ready to take me to Noodles for lunch a few minutes later, I throw my purse triumphantly over my shoulder, snag my coat and the chocolates—I consider the latter a parting settlement—and don't give Lisa a second glance when she asks where I'm going.

"I'm so proud of you!" Dena says, giving me a big squeeze, which is a little difficult in the small booth we're wedged in. "Tell me *exactly* what you told them." Her eyes glisten with excitement as I retell the story in great detail.

Summer's busy coloring in a book Dena wisely brought for her, but she echoes her mother's sentiments with, "All right, Aunt Kimmy!"

I sit back, lifting my chin with pride.

Dena lifts her brows. "And now the clock starts."

My pride fades. Her words sound ominous. "What clock?"

She gives a casual flick of her hand. "The clock for re-employment. You'll have to get right on it. It's a good thing you're covered through the first of the year. That way, you won't have to deplete your savings. It'll give you time to look for a new job."

My stomach turns at the thought of job searching. "Right. I'll have to get right on it."

"I can help. We can look through the paper and scour the Internet together. Find your perfect fit."

"Sounds great." I try to muster some enthusiasm.

Just then the waitress arrives and Dena orders a child's lasagna for Summer, a grilled chicken sandwich for herself, and asks what I want.

I glance through the menu. "I guess a chef's salad with ranch dressing on the side and the minestrone soup." True, it's a little late to start eating healthily, but I figure I should try to nab all the vitamins and minerals possible. Minestrone soup and salad probably have everything I need. Maybe the ranch counts as dairy.

"You almost make me feel guilty for my sandwich," Dena says once the waitress disappears with our menus.

I shrug, trying to look careless. "Don't be. It's just a new diet I'm trying out." Ugh. How do I tell her I'm pregnant? I want to tell her, but the words freeze on my tongue.

As I mull over my words, a pregnant woman passes our table with her husband in tow. She has one of those enviable pregnancies: a drum-tight basketball belly on a size-4 frame.

Knowing that I'll never be that small, pregnant or not, I hope people will eventually be able to tell that I'm carrying a baby and not a spare tire.

I can't control my body, but I *will* control my destiny!

For once, thinking about the coming months brings a determined smile to my face. *I can do this. I can find a job. Try to go back to school. People have done it before and succeeded. I can do it too.*

A small glow flickers to life in my heart. It spreads to my fingertips, filling me with an unfamiliar strength.

When the waitress returns with our meals, Dena and Summer dive into their respective sandwich and pasta, both of which smell so delicious that my mouth waters. But instead of asking for a bite, which I desperately want to do, I peel apart the bread and gingerly soak up my soup, knowing that I'm doing this for the coming baby. Nothing else would have made me surrender my usual order of stuffed manicotti.

It's as I'm drinking a glass of ice water that a sudden pain shoots through my abdomen. I gasp and bring a hand to my stomach. *What was that?*

Just when I think that I've imagined it, there it is again: a burning fist of fire clutching down inside me. "Ouch, ouch," I moan, gripping my belly.

"What's wrong?" Dena asks, straightening when she sees my face. "Kim? You okay?"

Something warm seeps between my legs. On reflex, I reach down and touch myself. When I hold up my fingers, they're tipped in dark blood.

Dena sees my hand. "Are you on your period?"

"No." My throat closes in. "I'm pregnant."

"What?"

"Pregnant," I say again, louder this time. I moan and hug myself.

"Okay, okay." Dena slides out of the booth and motions for me to follow. "Come on, Kim. We have to go."

"God, this hurts," I say, knowing this is worse than any period cramp I've ever experienced.

"I'll get the car." Dena fumbles for her wallet and tosses two twenties onto the table. She takes my hand and eases me out, then turns to Summer, who sits dumbstruck. "Come on, sweetie. We have to go."

Summer says nothing, only stares at me in fear as Dena guides us through the restaurant.

Tears are coursing down my face as I bite back another cry of pain.

"Stay calm, Kim. Just breathe." Dena pulls the door for me and holds it open with her foot. "You're going to be okay."

"What's wrong with me?" I seize her arms as another monstrous cramp rocks me. "Is it the baby?"

Dena doesn't answer, but her eyes say everything—and I can't stop the racking sobs.

Chapter Twenty-Five

"How do you feel?" Dena asks as sits at the edge of my bed.

I sway with the vertigo of our positions—reversed from so many years ago. Through the curtains, I catch sight of a man struggling under the weight of an enormous flower and balloon set, probably for his wife that just delivered their baby.

My chest tightens. No baby for me. No happy husband. No flowers or balloons. Now I have nothing. *Nothing.*

Darkness threatens to choke me, and I swallow hard and turn to my sister, remembering that she'd asked me a question. "I don't know," I answer finally. "It's like I'm in a fog."

Once again I'm in a paper nightgown, but this time I'm in an emergency room hospital bed with a heart monitor attached to my index finger that beeps on a machine to my right. Dena had rushed me here and used her license to get us seen quickly and then—well, to be honest, after that, it's all a haze. I remember being guided into a wheelchair and a doctor looking between my legs, a nurse drawing blood, a dark room where strangers in lab coats pressed wands into my body, waiting for a heartbeat that never came. The tears fell silent and hard, pooling into my ears long before the doctor explained how my body had failed me.

As the fog drifts, an aching numbness spreads. It's reminiscent of when I heard my mother died. First shock, then tears, then an empty void.

"I'm really sorry," Dena says, stroking my forehead.

My dry eyes pound with my pulse.

There's a long silence as we listen to the sounds of strangers in nearby beds, the drawing of curtains, and medical staff bustling past us, before Dena says, "You know, over a quarter of pregnancies end in miscarriage. Nothing you did could have prevented this."

I try to swallow a hard lump in my throat, but it's still there. I don't want to know about statistics, or what she read in medical school, or about any of her friends who've experienced this. I just want to be out of here, rewind to a few days ago.

When I found out I was pregnant, I was terrified. But then I accepted it and grew to want the baby. Now there is nothing, as if it never was. A part of me wishes this had never happened so that I wouldn't have to experience loss. *Again.*

At twenty-six, I've lost my mother, my father, my only serious boyfriend, and now my baby. It's too much and I'm feeling so sorry for myself that I almost can't breathe.

Dena opens the starched white blanket tucked around my legs and crawls in beside me, pulling my body close to hers. "Oh, Kimmy. I'm so sorry."

I let her hold me, crying onto her shoulder just like when we were kids, all those years ago. She strokes my hair and whispers soft, comforting words. My sobs fade, leaving me dried up and truly empty.

Dena kisses my clammy forehead. "It'll be okay."

"I miss Mom," I say, not knowing how much until just then.

"I know. Me too."

I shudder hard as Dena holds me. My muscles cramp with exhaustion, sadness, and renewed anger. *Why does this have to happen to me? To lose something that I love all over again?*

I suddenly wonder when Dena will die. Or if I will die first? Or will Summer suffer a horrible car accident like Mom? I'll have to endure more loss—and more if I ever find love again. Life seems so pointless, an endless track of pain and loss. It almost makes me want to give up and join my mother in Heaven, if there even is such a place.

My nurse returns with Summer, and my niece looks so scared for me it breaks my heart. "Come here," I say, and she climbs into bed with her mother and me. Soon we are all a tangle of limbs and breath, and slowly the emptiness gives way to something else: acceptance.

"Can I get you anything?" the nurse asks us hesitantly.

"We're fine," Dena answers, and the woman nods and shuts the curtain.

"Are you okay?" Summer asks, her bright eyes glimmering with unshed tears.

I force a smile and kiss her forehead. "I'm getting better, sweetie. Sorry if I scared you."

"I don't want to see you so sad," she says, hiccuping with tears.

"It's okay." I pull her to me. "It'll be okay."

"Shhh, honey," Dena soothes, kissing her. "We're all okay."

Summer exhausts herself and falls asleep within minutes. As I stroke her hair, I long for more days with her. How unfair that they'll soon leave, right when I need them most. At the same time, I know they must. Their life can never be mine.

"Are you going to tell Jared?" Dena whispers across to me.

I hesitate, thinking her question over, and finally shake my head. "He didn't even know I was pregnant."

Dena nods and we lay in silence for a while. My heart monitor beeps steadily beside us and I watch it for a while. "Is that a good heartbeat?" I ask her.

Dena glances at the monitor. "Sure. Very normal." There's an awkward pause, and I know that whatever follows will not be easy for her. "Kim, what were you going to do with a child?"

My body stiffens at the word *child*. "What do you mean?"

"You just quit your job. You broke up with Jarcd. What were you going to do?"

I reach to smear away a tear that's drying on my cheek. "I'd raise it, Dena. Just like you did Summer."

"But that was different. I had help. You're not in an easy position—"

But I cut her short, "I've never had it easy, Dena. Neither of us has. Truthfully, I was terrified when I found out. But then..." I sigh. "Then I just accepted it. I told myself I was pregnant, and that was it. I would raise the child and love it. That was all."

"You're so..." She is about to say more when she abruptly stops.

"What, Dena?" Even I hear the defensiveness edging my voice.

"Brave," she finishes, which takes me by surprise. Her smile is a mixture of sadness and pride. "You're so much braver than I am."

"I don't see how." I shake my head in protest. "You've done so much with your life. I've been stuck in this purgatory for years."

"No," she says firmly. "I ran away. I ran away from everything: my feelings, my friends, even you. When Mom died, I had to get away from anything that reminded me of her. I threw myself into my career and never looked back." She wipes her eyes. "But you never stopped talking about her, never stopped remembering. You do her memory more justice than I ever have."

"That's not true, Dena—"

"It is. And it's okay. I know it's true. I've just been such a coward."

"But you're talking about her *now*. You're remembering her. Maybe it was just something you had to give yourself time for in order to heal."

Dena smiles and sweeps the hair from my face. "I love you, Kim. I do."

"I know you do."

"I want us to be better. I want us to be friends."

"Me too," I say, meaning it.

Summer stretches in her sleep and I chuckle and lean down to kiss her forehead.

"I wish I could have a daughter like her," I say, wondering if I ever will.

"In a way you do," Dena says. "She'll always be your niece. Summer's a part of your life. She's your family."

My throat closes. *Family. Dena and Summer and I. A fresh set of musketeers.*

Dena's mobile rings and the two of us jump. Murmuring an apology, Dena pulls the phone from her purse and her eyes widen when she sees the number.

"Jonathan?" I ask immediately.

She nods. "Should I answer it? Maybe I shouldn't—"

"Answer it," I order, pushing the phone towards her. "It's important that you do. For you and Summer."

Dena hesitates another few moments. Then, just before the call goes to voicemail, she slips from the bed and steps past the curtain. "Hello, Jonathan..."

I settle back against the pillows. What would Jared say if he knew? Actually, he'd probably be relieved. He never wanted to marry me. Not really.

I'm just drifting off to sleep when the curtain pulls back. I startle awake, expecting Dena or my nurse, but am shocked and happy to see Jillian instead.

"What *happened*?" she demands, hastily lowering her voice when she sees Summer slumbering beside me. "I got this garbled message from your sister saying you were in the hospital!"

Dena called Jillian? How did she even find her number? Once again, I'm impressed by my sister's resourcefulness. I pat the space on the bed. "It's okay. Sit here."

Jillian crawls in beside us, and I quickly fill her in. She nods and says nothing, and soon the story is over.

"I can't believe you're pregnant," Jillian says at last. "Why didn't you tell me?"

"*Was* pregnant," I correct her. "And don't feel bad. I didn't tell anybody." My hand unconsciously travels to my stomach, still sore, but now empty. It's hard to believe that a life had existed there. Will it ever again?

"I'm so sorry," Jillian says. "I—I would have brought flowers or something. Maybe roses? White roses? I can get you some." She rises from the bed.

"It's okay," I say, stopping her. "It's fine."

She looks around. "How long will you be here?"

"Not long." I ease my pinned arm from beneath Summer's head. "Probably a few more hours. They ran some tests that should be back soon."

"But you're healthy otherwise?"

"As far as we know."

"That's good. I got so scared when I heard the message. I thought something terrible had happened. Like..." Her voice trails as tears fill her eyes.

"It's okay," I say, covering her hand with mine. "Nothing like that happened." I'm astounded to be surrounded by three people who love me, who genuinely care about my health and happiness.

Maybe I am lucky, despite everything.

The door opens, and Dena appears clutching her phone.

I perk up. "How did it go?"

She shakes her head as she angles the phone. "I think it'll be okay. He actually wants to talk to you—" She stops, noticing Jillian. "Oh hello! I see you got my message."

"I did." Jillian squares her shoulders. She's heard stories about my sister—mostly bad ones. "Although someone needs to teach you better skills at leaving messages. I thought Kimmy died!"

"Oh my god. I'm so sorry!" Dena shakes her head guiltily. "Sorry. I know Kim can attest to my lack of skills in that area."

"She sucks," I agree, accepting the phone from Dena. "Hello?"

"Kim?" calls Jonathan's deep voice over the line.

"Hi, John. How are you?"

"I'm good," he says. "Dena just told me what happened. I'm so sorry."

"Thanks." I draw a steadying breath. *I will be okay.*

"How do you feel?"

"A lot better now that everyone's here." I watch in amusement as Dena tries to engage Jillian—who's not quite certain what to make of her—in conversation.

"If there's anything I can do for you, let me know." And then he says something for my ears only and when he's done, I look over at my sister and my heart fills with happiness.

"Okay," I say. "Yes. I think that will work."

"Really? It's such a relief to hear you say that. Thanks."

"Would you like Dena back?"

"If you don't mind," he says and I return the phone to my sister.

Dena steps out of the room again and I watch her leave, my fingers unconsciously stroking Summer's hair.

"I take it you two are on the mend?" Jillian asks, looking quite surprised.

"You can say that."

"Well good. I'd say this was a long time coming."

"That it was," I say, gazing down at my niece. "You know what?"

"What?"

"I found out I was pregnant yesterday, and I lost the baby today." I sigh, unsure what to make of this.

"Fate," Jillian says at last.

"Fate?" I echo.

She nods and there's a brief pause. "You want to know what I think?"

I give her a look. "When have I ever wanted that?"

She smiles, hesitates a moment, and then plunges on, "Well, before you never really wanted kids and you sure weren't ready either. I think Summer gave you a taste of what it *could* be like to have a kid."

"What do you mean?"

"I mean, from what you tell me, when you found out you were pregnant, you mentally prepared yourself for having a baby, which is a very selfless thing. Maybe one day, when the time is right, you'll have a baby with someone worthy of you and everything will turn out great." She spreads her hands. "Call it what you want. Karma. God. Luck. I like to think of it as fate."

"Interesting," I say, wondering how fate could apply to me losing both of my parents. For the moment, however, it is so much more comforting to believe something like this is beyond my control. So I leave it at that. "Do you think you'll ever want kids?" I ask her.

"Sometimes." She looks down at Summer. "Other times I just want to get my tubes tied."

I chuckle. "That's why you're my best friend."

"Why's that?"

"Because no matter what, you can always make me laugh." It's as I say this that I realize this was something Jared could never do. In fact, all he ever did was leave me sad.

Maybe it's fate. All of it. Summer. My sister. Even Lisa. All steps to make me see my life for what it is and to go beyond it.

"You know what?" I ask, looking up at Jillian. "Fate doesn't sound like a bad idea after all."

Chapter Twenty-Six

FRIDAY, DECEMBER 23, 2005

Summer and I are just returning from a matinee when I notice a familiar car in my apartment's parking lot.

"What's wrong?" Summer asks, grasping my hand as we climb the stairs. I had volunteered to babysit Summer while Dena finished her Christmas shopping. My sister's not made it home yet, which I had initially been excited about, until I'd noticed the car.

"I need you to go straight to my bedroom and play with your toys," I tell Summer as I reach for the key to my front door and shakily open it.

Jared's sitting on my couch with a dozen red roses spread across his lap and a wrapped present on the coffee table. "Kim!" he says, lurching to stand. "I'd hoped you'd be back soon."

"Go on and play," I say to Summer, who obediently disappears into my room. I wait until I hear the door close before I fold my hands over my hips and say, "Jared, what are you doing here?"

"I had to see you," he says, looking like a beaten puppy. "It's been nine days and you've not returned a single one of my calls."

"That's because I don't want to talk to you." I hold out my hand, palm upwards. "I need my spare key back."

"Kim—"

"*Now*," I say, stalking towards him.

He grudgingly wrestles the key off his keychain and hands it to me. I slip it into my purse without looking at him. "I wish you didn't hate me," Jared says, his voice low and pained.

"I don't hate you," I say, wishing he hadn't come. His presence weakens my resolve. I have to stay strong.

"Well, whatever it is, I can change. I promise you. You always said how much more loving you wanted me to be. Well, I can *be* that guy for you, Kim. I'm ready now."

He reaches out to embrace me, but I step away and cross my arms. "No, Jared. It's too late."

"How's it too late?" He picks up the flowers, holds them out to me. He looks so pitifully sincere standing there that I have to wonder if he loves me, truly, and for the first time.

No, I tell myself. *It's that he needs me.*

I realize now that loving someone and needing someone are two very different things, and this is something Jared may never comprehend. "It's too late," I tell him, my heart gripped with sadness and regret. "Too little, too late."

"You're not the same," Jared says with a sad shake of his head. "The old Kim would at least have given me a second chance."

"The old Kim gave you a second chance. And she was stupid. I won't be that girl anymore." I draw a shaky breath and push out the words. "I'm sorry, but it's over."

Jared puts up his hand, as if to stall me. "Before you say anything like that, at least open your Christmas present." He lifts it from the table.

"Come on, Jared—"

"Open it." His face is strained. He takes off his Razorback cap and sets it on the couch, something he does only rarely. It's almost like he's *trying* to look vulnerable.

"Jared—"

"Please." He pushes the box to me.

This may be the only way to get him out of here, so I obligingly sit across from him and draw the present into my lap.

"I hope you like it." He smiles anxiously.

I pull back the wrapping and a familiar pink box stares back at me. It's from the boutique where I used to work, where I first met him. Inside is a set of sexy black lingerie: a sheer bra with faux pearls studding the straps and a matching thong with an oversized pearl sewn onto the backside.

I hold up the underwear in disbelief. "A bra? Panties? Jared, do you even *know* me?"

"What do you mean?" He looks genuinely confused. "I thought—"

I give a short, pained laugh. This present means nothing. Our relationship has meant nothing. This whole thing was just a two-year mistake.

I return the box to him. "I can't take this."

"Why not?"

"This isn't me. It never was. I only have all this stuff because you kept giving it to me, but I never wanted it. Not really."

It's as I say this that I realize Jared has been trying to mold me into something I wasn't from the very beginning: an always-ready-for-sex, doting woman who would never ask him to get serious and forgive his sexual transgressions. His ideal girlfriend.

Now that I have shaken off that image, Jared and I are like oil and water, so disparate in our natures that we can never mix.

Maybe Jillian is right. Maybe all of this is fate. I used to think such ideas were bullshit, but right now I find it unbelievably liberating.

I stand up and pass him the roses. "Take these and go. It's over."

Jared pushes the flowers back to me and says in a rush, "I'm sorry I cheated on you. I *am*. But can't you forgive me? It's over with Lisa. *Over*. If you want to know the truth, she seduced me. I had absolutely nothing—"

"I don't want to hear this!" I take three long strides away from him, to the front door, and open it. "No excuses. Nothing. Stop making this so hard and just go."

He stands there for a long time, his expression flickering between genuine hurt and confusion. Maybe he loves me. But it's not the love I want. Not anymore.

"Keep the present," he says at last. "And the flowers. I don't need them." He pushes the roses back into my arms, and then he walks out of my apartment and out of my life.

I shut the door on our two years together. Just like that.

Like my mother and my baby: they're all gone forever.

When I call Jillian minutes later, she comes over with a cheap bottle of champagne and two flutes. "We're celebrating!" she cheers, popping the cork.

"What are we celebrating?" I ask half-heartedly. I glance at my bedroom, where Summer is playing with the Barbie figurines her mother had packed for the trip.

Jillian passes me a glass and fills both nearly to the rim. "To the end! Cheers!"

I clink her glass and take a dutiful sip, looking at her. Then, realizing what she's saying, I ask, "What do you mean, 'the end'? The end of what?"

"Our relationships!" she says merrily. "Jared for you and Adam for me."

"You broke up with Adam? Today?" I cannot believe this. She ended her affair with her married boss?

"No, silly," she says with an airy laugh. "I broke up with him *days* ago."

"But—but why didn't you tell me?" This was a serious relationship for her and she usually tells me everything—well, ever since she finally admitted she was having the affair.

Her smile fades as we sit alongside each other on the couch. "Honestly? You were having such a rough time that I didn't want to add my problems to it. But now that you've finally kicked out that rotten scumbag, we can celebrate!"

"Okay," I say, re-clinking my glass with hers and taking a hearty gulp. "How was the break-up? Who ended it?"

She glances away as she takes another sip of champagne. "I'm glad to say it was me. And before his wife ever found out."

"So she may never know." I stare off into the distance, listening to the effervescent bubbles pop in my glass. "Did you ever wonder how many affairs he had before you?"

"Before me?" She considers. "I'm sure lots. And who wants to be with a man who cheats on his wife? I may be the one he's interested in now, but what happens after five, ten years? Then I'm going to be the dupe." She sighs. "Ugh. I'm going to have to change jobs for sure."

"Really?"

She gives me a look. "Please. Like I said, when you shit where you eat, it ruins everything."

I give her a small smile. "If it's any comfort, I quit my job too."

She gasps. "No way! When?"

"Yesterday."

"You're kidding! And with the miscarriage on top of it?"

I wince. "Yeah. Let's just say it wasn't the best day of my life."

"Sorry." She strokes my arm and shakes her head, and I know from the look on her face that she is having a hard time absorbing all of this, too. "So, what will you do now?"

I shrug and take another swig. "I guess look through the want ads. Until then, I'll live off my savings."

"Good for you." She smiles encouragingly. "And if you need any money, I can always be your friendly ATM."

"No, no." I shake my head vigorously. "Let's hope it never comes to that."

Jillian laughs and holds up her glass. "Here's another toast: to both of us finding our perfect jobs. And," she adds with a wink, "our perfect men."

"I'll be happy with just the job, thanks." I clink her glass and finish the remnants of champagne.

Jillian refills our glasses, then plops down next to me again. "So."

"So."

"1 like the flowers." She gestures towards the glass vase that I'd filled with Jared's roses, thinking at the time that they were too pretty to throw away.

"Thanks." I pull Jared's Christmas present down from the kitchen table. "He got me this too."

"Nice." She lifts the bra from the tissue paper with her index finger.

"Yeah. But not for me."

She drops it back into the box. "But you can't blame him on that count. You worked at a lingerie store when you first met."

"It was a temporary job. And besides, he saw me in the underwear I liked before we got serious. It was never me."

"Oh look," she says, examining the bra again. "He left the price tag on!"

"So?"

"So, why not return this and exchange it for something else?"

"I honestly couldn't care less. If you want it, you can have it."

"No, no. How about I take this back and choose something that is you? I'm your best friend and—I might add—I have the best taste of anyone you know."

"No argument there," I say, brightening. "Okay. Sure."

"Great." Jillian closes the box and slides it back on the table. "It's been a hectic couple of weeks for you, hasn't it?"

"For both of us." I swirl my flute and watch the bubbles spin like a miniature tornado.

"So, have you given any more thought to college?"

"I have, actually." I set down my glass and fold my legs under me. "I think it's something I may actually do."

"Good for you, sweetie!" Jillian gives me a big hug, though is careful not to tip her flute.

"I met a woman on campus recently. She almost finished with a lit degree. She's non-traditional, but seemed really happy with her choice to go back."

"Does she work as well?"

"On weekends. *And* she has a daughter."

"Wow," Jillian says, finishing her drink in one swift gulp. "That can't be easy. I remember barely scraping through some of my classes and I only had my own sorry ass to account for."

I nod. "It is something to consider. Money is always a factor."

"Well, you know what they say."

"What?"

"Educational debt is the best debt to get into."

I laugh. "You mean the only one you can't bankrupt! People should avoid all debt."

"True," Jillian concedes, "but I think investing in education differs from, say, going into debt for a pair of strappy Blahniks. Plus, with a higher education, you can find a better job and pay it off more quickly."

"Let's hope so."

"So, do you know what you'll major in?"

I shake my head. "Please. I'm just beginning to know myself."

Before Jillian can reply, the front door opens and Dena spills inside, clutching half a dozen stuffed shopping bags.

"Hey!" I say, standing up to help her. Jillian sets down her glass and we help ease the purchases onto the kitchen table. "You had quite a day, huh?" I ask, surveying.

"Got everyone done," Dena says with a satisfied sigh. "But no peeking. Some of yours are in there." Her gaze falls on Jared's roses. "Nice flowers."

"It's a long story," I say and roll my eyes.

Jillian picks up her purse. "Well, I better get going,"

"You don't have to leave!" I protest. "Besides, you still have half a bottle of champagne left."

She waves a dismissive hand. "It's fine. You keep it. I have to buy a few Christmas presents, anyway. Thanks for the inspiration, Dena."

"Sure thing!" she says brightly. "Just stay clear of any toy store. It's a madhouse in there."

Jillian barks a laugh. "No problem there. I'll call you later, Kim." And with that, she opens the door and disappears.

"Where's Summer?" Dena asks as she stacks her gifts into neat little piles.

"Playing with her toys. I'll go check on her." I stride to my bedroom and find my niece sitting on the carpet with a pile of Barbie clothes on her right, a Ken and Barbie doll in each hand, and a small pink convertible in front of her. "Hey, sweetie. Having fun?"

"Uh huh," she says, taking little notice of me.

"Your mom's outside. You want to play with us out there?"

"Okay." She gathers everything into her arms and struggles to stand.

I take the convertible and a handful of doll clothes and set everything beside the living room couch. Summer arranges herself at its center and quickly absorbs herself in fantasy.

"She's being so good," Dena observes. "She's really happy here."

I'm practically glowing with pride. "Thanks. But with your toys and movies, how could she not be?"

Dena laughs and eyes the half-empty bottle of Asti. "Mind if I have some?"

"Not at all." I open the overhead kitchen cabinet, grab a tumbler, and run it under the tap to clear out the ring of dust. "Sorry, no real stemware here."

"No problem," she says as I pass her the glass. She pours out more champagne. "Cheers."

"Cheers." We take a simultaneous sip. My eyes turn to the roses and I say, "I suppose you're wondering about the flowers."

"Don't tell me," she says, studying me carefully. "Jared?"

"How did you know?"

She shrugs. "Typical male. Did he try to win you back? And, more importantly, did you fall for it?"

"You'll be proud," I begin with a tired smile. And I tell her everything, leaving out no nuance or spoken word. She listens and nods appropriately and when I'm done, she smiles and embraces me.

"You did good, honey."

"Thanks." I smile at her, hesitate, and then ask, "So how are you doing with Jonathan? Is it any better?"

Her smile fades. "I think so. He's going to call me tomorrow. He's been researching couples counselors, and we'll start going after the New Year. I'm thrilled he's taking the initiative on this. Anyway, we had a long talk and we're both going to be better. Not just for

Summer, but for all of us." She swipes the hair from her wet eyes. "We really do love each other."

"I know you do," I say, for once not envying my sister for this, but am genuinely glad. Relieved, even.

She shrugs. "Time will tell. It's still undecided if we'll be able to spend Christmas with each other."

"Really?"

"I'm afraid so. It's the season to fly and all tickets are almost gone. Luckily, I could adjust my flight here." She sighs. "I don't know. Hopefully, it'll work out."

"It will," I say. "Come on. Let's watch some TV."

We sit on the couch and tune into *Law & Order*, which we watch straight into the commercial with hardly any words spoken. I think we're both thinking of the past few days, how much has happened and how much is changing. And all before the New Year.

Suddenly a commercial appears featuring Cindy Crawford. The leggy model smiles seductively at the camera and runs a hand through her trademark brunette tresses, looking perfect.

My stomach tightens as I glance at my niece. "Summer?"

She meets my eyes with bright curiosity. "Hmmm?"

"Do you love me? Even a little?" I hold my breath, not sure why I've asked her this. It's not like I *want* to drag a compliment from a six-year-old. I just need a tad of reassurance. Not from a man. And not from my best friend or sister.

Summer glances first at me, then at the television. She shakes her head.

"Summer!" Dena exclaims, clearly mortified. "You say you're sorry!"

My heart sinks. "It's okay," I say, because I know, given time, Summer will love me, or at least I hope she will. All that matters is that I love her now as much as I've loved anyone. And I know that she'll be in my life forever, because I will always try to be there for her.

"I love you more than a little, Aunt Kim," says Summer, her eyes bright as she opens her arms very wide, as if she's trying to hug the world. "I love you *this* much!"

Tears spring to my eyes. Kneeling beside my niece, I fall into an embrace better than any I thought possible.

Chapter Twenty-Seven

On Christmas Eve, Summer sits squeezed between Dena and me on my couch. Together, we sip hot chocolate from steaming ceramic mugs and watch A Charlie Brown Christmas. True to the Kincaid tradition, all the presents are beneath the Christmas tree in organized piles, waiting expectantly for tomorrow morning's unwrapping.

As Summer giggles at the holiday cartoon, I wait for the inevitable knock on my front door. When it finally comes, I nearly leap out of my skin from excitement.

"Can you get that?" I ask Dena, pretending I have to go to the bathroom. But I stop after I've taken a few steps, watching my sister unlock the door and open it.

"Merry Christmas, honey!" Jonathan says, his breath coming out in great white puffs as he reaches forward to embrace my sister.

Dena lets out a surprised gasp and Summer squeals and bounds from the couch. "Daddy!"

"Hey, pumpkin." He kneels down to hug her. "How are you?"

"I missed you!" she cries, burying her face in his black wool coat, her arms spread wide across him.

"What are you doing here?" Dena asks, surprise and happiness lacing her voice.

"I couldn't spend Christmas Eve away from you guys." He grins at both of them before finally looking at me. "Hey, Kim."

"Hi, Jonathan." In four steps, I'm hugging him too. His cheeks are like ice and I shoo him inside and close the door.

"But—how?" Dena stammers, helping him out of his coat.

"I took the first flight here," he explains. Then, reaching into his inside jacket pocket, he removes a set of envelopes. "For you."

Dena's hand flies to her mouth when she opens the first. An airline ticket home. "*Jonathan!*"

"What is it?" Summer asks, jumping up and down. "Lemmie see!"

Dena turns to me, a smile tugging at her lips. "Did you know about this?"

"Maybe," I say, throwing Jonathan a conspiratory wink.

"But, Jonathan," she says. "I thought—"

"I'm taking you home for Christmas," he says, pulling her to him. "No matter what, we have to spend Christmas together as a family." He glances at me and laughs. "And don't think I'm leaving you out of this, Kim."

"What do you mean?" I say, not privy to this part of the plan.

"He has one for you too," Dena says, handing me an envelope.

I take it from her and there it is. In crisp black ink is my name with a first-class stamp all the way to New Jersey.

"You're spending Christmas with us," Jonathan says, his tone firm yet jocular. "No way I'm letting you stay here alone."

It's been five years since I've spent Christmas with Dena and back then, all we did was bicker until we stopped speaking. Jonathan tried his best to play referee, but there was nothing he could do for us: our anger and resentment came long before him, spinning back into our childhood. Since then I've been with Jared or Jillian or friends of friends. This will be the first truly joyful Christmas that I spend with family in almost a decade. "Thank you," I say, reaching up to kiss Jonathan's cheek. "This means so much."

"You're welcome." Suddenly he looks serious, and glances briefly at my now-empty belly. "Listen, I'm really sorry about—"

"It's okay," I say, not wanting to think about that, not now. I just want to hold on to this happiness for as long as possible. "Honestly. It's okay."

Jonathan nods and then turns to everyone else and proclaims, "Let's get going. The plane leaves in three hours. Our first order is to pack these presents."

"But we have too much stuff," I say, gazing down at the spread of presents beneath my tree in sudden despair.

But Dena laughs and shakes her head. "Honey. It's first class. Pack as much as you want. Welcome to a whole new world of travel."

In a mad rush of excitement, we pack all our bags and pile them into the awaiting cab. As I struggle to arrange our luggage in a real-life version of Tetris, a familiar voice calls, "Are you moving out too?"

I turn to see Alice coming down the stairs with Brandon walking behind her with a box under his arm.

"I'm spending Christmas with my sister in New Jersey," I reply, my voice bubbling with excitement. *I'm spending Christmas with my sister! And my niece! And my brother-in-law! At their fabulous new house! And I'm actually looking forward to it!*

"How wonderful!" Alice says. She extends her hand to Dena. "You must be her sister."

I give quick introductions before asking Alice, "What are you doing here?"

"Just saying goodbye to the other neighbors."

I shake my head in wonder. Alice would be the type of person to know the other neighbors.

She smiles warmly at me. "You have my new contact info, right?"

"I do." She'd slipped it under my door a few days ago.

"Great. Well, I won't keep you. Have a wonderful Christmas. Goodbye, Summer," Alice says, smiling down at my niece.

"I'll call you," I say, hoping that when I return, we can become even better friends.

"You better." She reaches out to hug me. "Have a wonderful time."

I look at Brandon and he smiles at me, but it's a different smile than from before. Does he know I broke up with Jared? I notice his eyes look especially blue today. I smile back and try not to blush.

"We better go," Jonathan says, and Summer yanks at my arm.

We load ourselves into the cab and start up the road; the wind whipping into the car's bumper as the trees flanking us sway from the weight of the ice.

"Who was *he*?" Dena asks, looking at me pointedly.

"Just a friend," I say, but inside I thrill at the possibility of seeing him again. But I decide to keep this part to myself. For now, anyway.

So here I am sipping champagne for the second time in two days, lounging in a first-class leather armchair on my way to New Jersey. It's almost like I'm suspended in a dream, giddy with unforeseen happiness.

To show off my new purchases, as well as to put them to use

since I'm now out of a job, I'd changed into my navy suit and creamy camisole. Now I actually fit in with the business elite that inhabit the cabin. I am nearly unrecognizable from who I was last year, or even a few weeks ago. Gone is the mousy hair, the blue eye shadow and black lipstick. While I'm nowhere near gorgeous, at least I look put-together. Dare I say elegant?

"You look amazing," Dena says, smiling over at me as Summer sleeps with her face pressed against the side of my arm with her stuffed brown puppy clutched to her chest. "Looking like that, you could land any job you want."

"Thanks," I say, hoping that's true. Over the past hour, we'd discussed the careers I've admired in my lifetime. I really like physical therapy. It takes nowhere near the schooling necessary to become a medical doctor, but I could still help tons of people and the pay is so much better than secretarial work. I've also thought about joining Jonathan and Frieda in the teaching ranks. I imagine myself in front of a packed auditorium lecturing about—what? I'm not great at anything in particular, but I can learn. While my options aren't limitless, they still stretch further than they ever have before.

I think about all of this as I sip the chilled champagne. It's Christmas Eve. I have no job, no man, no parents, and no baby, but I have my family now, and hope. If there's ever been a Christmas wish, it is this.

"You look happy," Dena observes, breaking my reverie.

"I do?"

"Yes. In fact," she says, looking at me closely, "I've never seen you look happier."

"You probably haven't," I say, smiling. "And maybe it's catching. You look happy too."

Dena smiles and lowers her eyes to her hand that is laced with Jonathan. Like his daughter, he's fast asleep. Unlike his daughter, he's snoring. "I'm getting there," says Dena eventually. "I'm getting there."

"Summer!" I call from the balcony. "Come see this!"

"What?" She races to me, tugging her coat closed and holding on tightly to her stuffed dog.

"This." I pick her up and balance her between my stomach and the wooden ledge of Dena's second story home. We arrived a half-hour before and now Dena and Jonathan are unpacking. But I couldn't unpack just yet: I had to explore. This is the first time I've been to their new house and I'm dumbstruck by its beauty. Its two stories with a full basement converted into a gym and "man cave", four spacious bedrooms, and a gorgeously landscaped backyard. Suffice it to say: my dream house.

It's too cold for legitimate exploring, but from here I can see everything: the broad oak and pine trees, a periphery of trimmed shrubberies, and allegedly a full garden beneath the thick snowfall. And although I can see the neighboring houses, they're not flushed against the side of the house. There's space. Room to breathe.

Behind us are about two acres of rolling hills and woods. And in the distance is the most spectacular sunset I have ever seen. The sky is the color of burnt orange, with splashes of crimson and yellow gold. Crisp white contrails feather across the sky to mingle with the wispy cirrus clouds overhead. A gust of cold air blows in from the west, but I hold Summer close and we watch the sunset together, something I haven't done since I was a child.

"Why does it have all those colors?" Summer asks, staring out in awe.

"I don't know." My mind tickles with facts and figures from

high school—air pressure, stratosphere, something scientific—but I push these thoughts away and just appreciate it for what it is.

When the colors dim to black, I kiss Summer's forehead and help her to the ground. "Thanks so much for letting me take care of you these past two weeks, kiddo."

"At first you didn't want to," she says, grinning.

"Well, neither did you," I remind her.

She giggles. "Oh yeah. I forgot."

I laugh and ruffle her hair. "It was a surprise. But I'm sure glad it happened."

"Me too." She reaches out to hug my knees.

A tide of emotion washes over me. "I love you," I tell her.

"I love you, too."

I stroke her forehead and gaze down into her bright eyes, hoping one day I can have a child just like her. "I promise that I'm going to be the best aunt you'll ever have."

"But you already are!" she says.

"But even better. This year is a new start for us." I extend my hand. "Deal?"

"Deal," she says, and shakes it.

Chapter Twenty-Eight

I can't sleep. Santa has come. I creep into Dena's bedroom and she is not awake. I lean over the cool covers and shake her shoulders.

"Mmmm," she moans, turning away from me.

I yank back the covers and slip into the sheets that are warmed by her body. "Dena! Wake up! It's Christmas!"

"Kimmy," she says, irritated. "I'm asleep!"

"It's Christmas! Get up!"

"Why?"

"Because you *have* to." I won't admit the truth: that the dark halls and empty spaces send a chill through me.

"Five minutes." She pulls a pillow over her head.

I decide that I have to bargain with her, so I lean in very close and say, "I'll let you open the first present."

There's a pause. Gradually, she lowers the pillow and opens her bleary eyes. "You want to open gifts that badly, huh?"

"Yes, yes!" I bounce on my knees.

Dena's body rocks to my rhythm. A slow smile creeps across her face. "Okay, Miss Persistence. I'm up."

"Yay!" I say, but do not move until she is out of bed. Then, taking a few steps ahead of her, I lead the way to Mom's room.

I push the door open into a draft of cool air. Then—bare toes creaking the floorboards—I slink to Mom's bedside and lean over to see if her eyes are open. But she's asleep. She looks so peaceful that I wonder if I should wake her. But my need to open gifts overrides any further hesitation. "Mami," I whisper, then louder, "Mami!" When she doesn't move, I jump up, pull myself onto the bed, and place feather-light kisses onto her cheeks and forehead.

Her eyelids pinch closed as she yawns. "Hmmm? Wha—?"

"It's Christmas," Dena announces, laughing. "Kimmy wants us all up."

"Oh." Mom grins as she moves to hug me. "Merry Christmas, honey. All right, all right. I'm up."

I race down the stairs and kneel at the stacks of presents surrounding the tree, quickly scanning the tags to register which ones are mine. I smell coffee from the kitchen and in minutes Mom returns with a steaming cup balanced between her hands, laughing as Dena and I sort out the presents. "Here's one for you!" I cry, pushing a heavy, wrapped box across the floor towards Mom.

"My girls," she says, setting the cup beside her. "You both are so beautiful."

I beam. It's rare that I'm grouped in Dena's category. "Did you hear that?" I ask my sister in triumph.

"I did," Dena says, laughing with me.

"I think before we open any presents, we should all have a family picture." Mom stands and heads back into the kitchen.

My heart drops. "But the *presents*!"

"They can wait," she calls, returning shortly with her camera.

"I agree with Kimmy," Dena says. "It's freezing outside. And I think it just snowed."

"Then imagine how pretty it'll look in the picture." Mom smiles encouragingly. "Let's go. Boots and coats on. The sooner we do it, the sooner we can get back, okay?"

Dena and I drag our feet to the coat closet. Dena has to help me maneuver the zipper of my jacket and I pull on the red mittens that are shoved into the pockets. Mom opens the back door and I look out into our yard that is covered in sheets of ice and snow. Slowly we creep across the treacherous porch, Dena holding my arm as Mom follows close behind. "Over there!" Mom says, pointing to the old wooden bench that she'd recently purchased at a garage sale.

Dena and I take our seats. I look back at the house, wondering if Santa remembered the Barbie RV I'd described in my letter to him.

"Well, this won't work," Mom says, looking about for something to put her camera on.

"Why don't you put it on the edge of the bench?" Dena suggests, blowing hot air into her reddening hands. "It's wide enough to support it."

"Good idea." Mom angles the camera so that Dena and I—now standing a few feet away—fit into the frame. "Smile, girls!" she says, then pushes the timer.

We smile dutifully as Mom fits herself between us. Just as the flash goes off, Mom tickles our sides and Dena and I burst out laughing.

"That will be lovely," Mom says, smiling at us. "*Feliz Navidad, mis hijas.*"

Dena smiles. I look up at my mom and sister and say, "Present time?"

"Yes, yes." Mom sighs, but she is still smiling. "Present time. Merry Christmas, Kimmy."

"Yeah. You too!" I say, already forgetting my promise to Dena as I rush back inside to tear open the first present.

Chapter Twenty-Nine

"Santa came! Santa came!" Summer cries, bounding into my guest room and leaping upon my bed. "Wake up, Aunt Kim! Santa came!"

"Five more minutes," I grumble, pulling the comforter over my eyes.

"No, no!" she exclaims, giggling as she places rapid-fire kisses over my cheeks and forehead. "Now! Mommy and Daddy are already looking at the presents."

"Then what are you doing here?"

"Getting you up, silly." She rolls her eyes as she helps me out of bed and into a pair of slippers.

We stroll downstairs together, hand-in-hand. Dena meets us at the landing and hands me a steaming mug of coffee. "Good morning, sister," she says, and then gives me a kiss on my cheek. "Merry Christmas."

"Merry Christmas," I say, kissing her back. "I seem to remember you had a fondness for sleeping in on Christmas morning. What changed?"

"Having a kid," she says, and we laugh at the truth of this.

I follow Dena into the living room, where a nine-foot Christmas tree makes my Douglas fir look the size of a toothpick. "I decorated it myself," Jonathan says proudly.

Summer and I notice the haphazard arrangement of bulbs, lights, and tinsel and exchange looks with a secret grin. I slip onto a crisp leather couch, careful not to spill my coffee as I take my first few sips. Jonathan leaves to turn on some Christmas music and soon "Carol of the Bells" floats down from unseen speakers.

"Aunt Kim first!" Summer exclaims, picking up a wide present and dragging it over to me.

"No, Summer." Dena puts up a hand. "That's from Mommy. I want her to open that last."

"Okay," Summer says, traipsing to the pile and returning with another gift.

"Thank you, sweetie," I say, kissing her.

"That's from Summer," Dena says with a wink. "She picked it out herself."

"You did, huh?" I lift the small present into my lap and rip off the paper. Inside is a Burberry perfume I know cost well over my fifty-dollar budget. It's something I've always wanted for myself but knew it was too expensive to buy. "Thank you, Summer," I say, then stand and embrace my sister. "You really shouldn't have. It's too much."

"It's nothing," she says, shooing me away. "And you've got lots more to go, so you better reserve your hugs until the end."

Summer passes out the gifts like a miniature Santa Claus and we open them amongst boisterous conversation. My sister and brother-in-law make a big deal over my gifts to them, but of course the most ecstatic is Summer, who clutches her ivory unicorn to her chest like a child possessed, which thrills me endlessly.

I think about what Christmas would have been like had I not taken care of Summer: I would still be with Jared, still be working my meaningless job, still unhappy. Sitting here with my family and presents and a hot mug of coffee—it still seems so surreal.

Finally, there's only one present left. Dena looks at me expectantly. "Open it," she commands.

"Do you know what's inside?" I ask Jonathan and Summer, but they shake their heads. It's heavy and square-shaped and I'm having a hard time figuring out what it is. Finally, I pull off the paper and the velvet back of a frame stares back at me.

"Other side," Dena whispers.

I turn it over, and my hands freeze on the glass. It's the picture of Mom, Dena, and me that I keep in my nightstand, blown up in meticulous detail. I'm in pigtails and Dena is wearing her favorite starburst pajama bottoms. Coats that were thrown out years ago are zipped to our chins.

Mom looks so happy. So *alive*. For a moment, I forget about her death, about the pain, and all the years of separation. Mom took this picture before any of that, when Dena and I were as close as two sisters can be. "Thank you," I say, tears stinging my eyes. "Thank you."

Dena comes over to embrace me. I can't stop my tears from seeping into her hair. She only grips me tighter.

"We'll leave you to it," Jonathan murmurs, guiding Summer into the kitchen.

Dena shifts in my arms. Her voice is barely a whisper. "I want us to be like this. Before everything."

"I'd like that," I say, gazing at the faded image of the three of us. The Three Musketeers. We were so happy once. It seems like centuries ago.

I wonder if it's possible to experience great tragedy and loss and still hold on to what you had before. Dena and I still have the strings of an almost-forgotten relationship, and we're trying to weave them together. And something tells me it will hold.

I think of all the friends and lovers that I've known in the nine years since our mother died. Now I have Dena, Jonathan, Summer, and Jillian. Four people, out of the hundreds I've met, that I can count on. And I'm making more friends, like Alice and Brandon. There's possibility there.

True, I have no job and no man in my life and my future stretches before me with no hint of its resolution. But even as I think about all these things, I find myself smiling.

Because I'm *choosing* to start over, and it's not nearly as scary as I once thought.

Epilogue

I stride to the counter at the University of Arkansas's registrar's office and smile at the woman who glances up from her computer.

"Hello," I say, placing my acceptance letter and crisp identification card onto the counter. "I'd like to sign up for classes, please."

Thank you for reading!

Like this book?
Please leave a review on Amazon/Goodreads.

Join Katherine's newsletter to stay up-to-date with new releases,
sneak peeks, giveaways, and more.

www.katherinetiradoryen.com

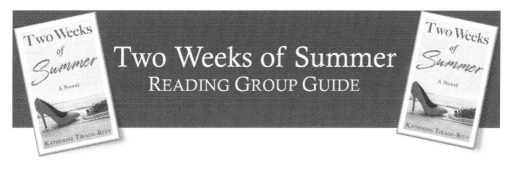

Two Weeks of Summer
READING GROUP GUIDE

1. The novel opens in a dress shop. How does this foreshadow future events? Do you relate to Kim's childhood experiences?

2. What was your initial impression of Kim? What about her boyfriend, Jared? Does their relationship have any redeeming qualities? Have you experienced a similar relationship?

3. Were you surprised by Kim's response to Summer's arrival? Why or why not? How does Kim adapt to this sudden responsibility?

4. Are Kim and Dena more alike or different? Support your reasoning with passages from the novel. Have you experienced a similar dynamic?

5. How do Kim's interactions with her coworker, Lisa, highlight Kim's broader issue with interpersonal relationships? Have you ever struggled with coworkers? Do you agree that Kim's should quit her job?

6. On a scale from healthy to toxic, how do you rate Kim and Jared's relationship? Apply the same rating scale to Dena, Jillian, and Alice.

7. Is Kim ready to become a mother? Why or why not? Support your opinion with passages from the novel.

8. Do the flashback scenes influence your opinion of Kim? How did a Puerto Rican heritage shape Kim and her family?

9. How did her mother's death impact Kim? Could you relate to Kim's loss? How does Kim grow and change in the novel?

10. Discussing books is sometimes almost as exciting as reading them. How would you describe *Two Weeks of Summer* to someone who has not read it? Would you recommend it to a friend or loved one? What do you imagine Kim doing next?

For more by Katherine Tirado-Ryen, visit
www.katherinetiradoryen.com

MEADOW LAKE PRESS

Printed in Great Britain
by Amazon

c2ab2b46-ebdd-46f3-b0f7-c3a6b54d2767R01